Bronze Not Gold

A Christian Mystery

D1528650

by Nancy Gooding

Also by Nancy Gooding

Books in The Restoration Series:
Sister From the Other Side
The Juniper Tree
Eye Of a Needle
Seduction of a Minor God
After the Storm
All We Like Sheep
A Seed Fell
Day of the Mockingbird

Books in The Garden of Grace Series:
The Ultimate Deception

More Books by Nancy Gooding:
Whispered Warnings
The Days Of Nimrod
The Days of Noah and The Nephilim

Children's Books:
The Terrible Dreads
Eyelashes on My Toes
A Friend for Bernice

Acknowledgements

A huge thank you to Lizzy Rainey for her painting and cover picture depicting the rescue. I also want to thank my editor, Rachel Leone, for her tireless work and encouragement. These two ladies along with all of you who have read the manuscript and graced me with your suggestions and corrections are special gifts to me. This book has reached fruition because of those who believed, prayed, and encouraged me not to give up.

Prologue

Jenna Harrison woke with a start and listened. *What was that sound?* It was familiar, she was sure. Her husband, sleeping peacefully beside her, rolled to his side.

Slipping from the bed, Jenna made her way to the kitchen. The moonlight streaming through the window gave the room an eerie feeling. Checking the knob on the back door, she sighed in relief. *Good, it's locked.*

She headed back to her bedroom but stopped. *Wait, why isn't Brenda's night light on?* Rushing to her daughter's room, she flipped on the light, pulled back the covers, and tried not to panic. Calling the child's name, she rushed to the front door and moved the knob back and forth. Good, the door was still locked, but screaming in her mind were the headlines of yesterday's newspaper.

Second Child Abducted

Raymond Harrison was standing up before he realized he wasn't asleep anymore. He caught Jenna by the wrist and stopped her as she passed him. Flying down the hall, she screamed Brenda's name.

"Just quiet down, she's here someplace," he said, trying to be rational.

Twisting out of his grasp she screamed, "No, she's not! Oh God, no! Please no!"

It took only a short time to search the five-room house. They frantically looked under every bed, every table, and behind the sofa all the while calling Brenda's name. Looking at each other in disbelief, she whispered, "Call the police."

With shaking fingers, he dialed the number posted over the telephone. Minutes later, sirens announced the arrival of three squad cars. The police officers were efficient and determined. They searched every inch of the house and yard. They pounded on the doors of frightened and curious neighbors. They checked every window and door for a break-in. All was to no avail. The house was locked up tight. Every window was locked, but two-year-old Brenda was gone. It couldn't be happening, not to them, but it was. Once again, a child disappeared into the night without a trace, and no one knew how or why.

Chapter One

Ellen Evans rolled over and squinted at the illuminated dial on her bedside clock. "Three-thirty," she moaned. She was troubled when she went to bed, and sleep was long in coming. Now she was awakened by sirens singing their worrisome song.

"Please, God, help whoever is in trouble," she whispered, but her concern for others soon reverted to her own problems. *What am I going to do? Please, God, I need answers.* Punching her pillow, Ellen kicked the covers off her feet, prayed for a miracle, and went back to sleep.

~~~

Early the next morning, Ellen hurried to the newsstand. Ignoring the headlines in big black letters of child abduction, she turned to the want ads. Scrutinizing the possibilities, she circled one that looked promising and headed back to her apartment to make the call.

The ad read: Light housekeeping in exchange for free room and board. An answering service took down her information. At first, the questions were familiar: previous employment, education, age, but then, height and weight. As the questions became even more personal, Ellen wondered briefly why her size and the color of her eyes and hair were important, but she ignored the warning flags.

As the interviewer promised, a man called within moments, but the offer was clear. He wanted a maid with benefits. Clicking off the phone, she sat glaring at the black hunk of plastic as if it were responsible for the insulting proposition and hollered toward the ceiling, "I prayed God! Where are you?"

Six months ago, Ellen had quit her job as a home economics teacher, packed up all of her belongings, and moved one hundred and eighty miles from everyone and everything familiar. It was a bit like jumping off a cliff, but at age thirty, she reasoned it was now or never. The year was nineteen sixty-two and women were beginning to feel their independence both politically and culturally. With dreams of liberation and fame, Ellen Evans accepted a job with Musgrave's Couture Bridal Salon, moved into a one-room apartment, and tried to keep her faith. Within a week, she realized her job description was misleading. Instead of designing wedding gowns as

4

promised, her job title was alterations coordinator. The owner of the shop, Marilyn Musgrave, had falsely described what she would be doing, and when she questioned her, she was told that every designer had to start at the bottom. Ellen soon began to lose heart.

It wasn't long before things began to look overwhelming. Ellen's apartment was too expensive for her salary and left much to be desired. While looking through the window with its perfect view of a rusty fire escape, she began to wonder why she had ever left home.

Sighing heavily, she dropped onto the dilapidated sofa that doubled as her bed and studied the bills accumulating on her coffee table. On top of everything else, the muffler on her eighteen-year-old car fell off yesterday, and car repairs were not in her budget.

She knew her mother would welcome her home with open arms, but sighed as she recalled their last conversation. *Mom, I love you, but I need to do this for me. I don't want to look back in thirty years and think...I could have been a designer, but I was too afraid to leave home.*

Deep in memory, she was startled by a knock on the door. Looking through the peephole, she saw it was Abby, her co-worker from the bridal shop.

Ellen opened the door and crowed, "Come in!"

"I hope I'm not interrupting."

"Are you kidding? You probably just stopped me from calling my mother!"

"And that's good?" Abby asked innocently.

"The call, oh my, yes," Ellen giggled. "Let's put it this way, my mother thinks I'm delusional. She can't understand why I'd leave the stability of teaching home economics and move so far away to chase a pipe dream."

"Hmm, designing wedding dresses."

"Yes," Ellen sighed. "Even though this job isn't what I expected, I guess I feel as if I've somehow escaped from jail."

Tilting her head, Abby frowned and tried to understand.

"My mother," Ellen explained.

"Your mother wants to put you in jail?" Abby asked, still confused.

"Maybe jail is a bit harsh."

"Controlling?" Abby questioned as the light went on.

"Yes, she means well, and I know she loves me, but she's never happy unless I live my life in what she considers acceptability. So yes, you've saved me! Do you want some company for breakfast?" Ellen asked, heading for the bathroom. "Just give me a minute to comb my hair and brush my teeth."

"Well, yes, but actually I came with a proposition." Abby plunked down on the sofa, distracted momentarily by the newspaper lying on the coffee table. "Have you been following these abductions?" she asked.

"I'm ashamed to say I haven't," Ellen called from the bathroom. "Give me a minute to put on some makeup."

"I think this is the third little girl that's been abducted. It's all so sad."

Ellen stood in the doorway of the bathroom, looking concerned, and twisted her hair into a ponytail. "Yes, it's terrible. I guess I didn't realize…but you said you came with a proposition?"

"If you're not interested, I'll understand. After all, you have your own place here and…"

"You want me to room with you?" Ellen interrupted hopefully.

"There are already three of us in the house, but we need four to pay the bills. You're probably not interested, but I just thought I'd ask. You would have your own room. It's a four-bedroom house, but you'd have to share the bathroom with me. It only has two bathrooms."

"Can I afford it?"

"Well, I don't know what you're paying here but…"

Ellen shot her a number.

"Oh, it would be half that."

Ellen caught her breath, "You're kidding!"

"I think the other girls will like you…except for Joan, but she doesn't ever like anyone. She's strange."

"Strange in what way?"

"Well, for one thing, she's all about the supernatural. She goes to this psychic. I think her name is Katrina Polworth."

"I've never heard of her."

"Just as well, but Joan thinks she is going to be rich and famous because Katrina read her future, and she said it's very clearly in the cards. Let's see, she either said she was going to be rich and famous or at least marry someone rich and famous. I can't remember, but you don't have to worry about her. She's hardly ever home."

"Well, I guess that's good."

"For sure. When she is home she's always in a bad mood. She has tried to talk me into going with her to a séance or to have my cards read or whatever they call it."

"I hope you said no."

"Well of course I said no. I don't believe in that kind of thing."

"I don't know much about it, but enough to stay away."

"You don't need to decide now if you want to think about it."

"Going to a séance?"

Abby laughed, "No, silly, moving in with me."

"Are you serious? Of course I want to move in with you!" Ellen laughed. "You don't realize what a miracle this is! Thankfully my landlady didn't make me sign a lease. I can leave next weekend."

"Great. Let's go for pancakes. I'll even buy!"

Chapter Two

It was the first warm day in March, and Anthony Sands was too busy pouring soapy water over his new, red Ford Fairlane to notice what was going on across the street. Concentrating on removing the drags of winter, it took him a while before he noticed four girls struggling with a trunk. He wondered briefly if he should offer to help them but decided against it.

He had often seen the blonde. With her bleached white hair and deep red lipstick, she was attractive in a Marilyn Monroe sort of way. He'd waved a few times, but she always ignored him.

The freckled redhead looked younger, maybe in her early twenties. She wasn't someone you would notice, but at least she was friendly, and she always smiled and waved.

Lois Collins was the third female. He knew her because she worked with his mother for Tate and Tate's Law Firm. Lois and his mother rode to work together. He had tried to be friendly in the past, but she was almost as rude as the blonde.

Although not beautiful, there was an air of mystery about her. She wore her short dark hair in an asymmetric haircut, was tall and thin, and always looked as if she was about to strike a pose for a fashion magazine. Aware of these three, he was paying them little mind, but then he noticed the fourth girl.

He was having second thoughts about offering to help when the new girl walked toward him. Her long black curly hair was pulled up tight on top of her head, but tiny curls escaped and framed her face.

As she got closer, he caught his breath…she was beautiful. Her large, pale blue eyes fringed with black lashes hypnotically caught his attention, and her warm smile melted any reserve he had managed to muster.

She extended her hand. "Hi, I'm Ellen Evans. I've just moved in," she motioned towards the house with her head. "Across the street."

"I'm Tony, uh, Anthony," he said, wiping his wet, soapy hand on his shirt before taking hers.

"Unusual name, Tony-uh-Anthony," she teased. "Listen, can you help me? I can't seem to lift my trunk and neither can my housemates," she laughed and motioned toward the other three. "If you could just help us maneuver it into the house, I would be eternally grateful."

He was embarrassed that she was forced to ask for help before he volunteered, and stammered, "Of course, of course." Turning off the water, he followed her.

"I hope your wife won't mind if we borrow you for a few minutes," she asked coyly, fishing for his status.

"Well, uh, no. Actually, I'm…I'm, well, my wife died a year ago."

"Oh, I'm so sorry!" She looked into his eyes with sincere concern.

The women waiting applauded as the two started walking towards them.

"Ellen found us a man!" Abby cheered.

The blonde gave him a cool smile and said, "Good, then you won't need me." Dropping her gaze, she hurried into the house. Lois sighed deeply but barely acknowledged him. With much heave-hoeing, the four managed to maneuver the trunk into what was soon to be Ellen's room.

They situated the trunk, and Ellen walked him to the door. "What can I do to repay you?" she asked with twinkling eyes. "Wouldn't a man living alone appreciate a homemade apple pie?"

"Well, I do appreciate the offer, but I don't live alone. My mother moved in to take care of me and my three-year-old daughter, Jennifer."

Their eyes locked in an awkward moment. She smiled and looked away, "Okay, well, I guess your mom probably makes better pies than I do anyway," she conceded with a smile. "What did you say her name is?"

"Judy, Judy Sands. Actually, she works with your roommate, Lois."

"I would like to meet her sometime. Maybe she can drop by for coffee."

"Yes, that would be nice," he said but continued standing there.

"Thanks again Tony-uh-Anthony."

He smiled at her teasing and then seemed to realize he was being dismissed. "Okay then, I'll see you around." He turned and headed back to his house.

"Yes, I sure hope so," she whispered to his retreating back.

~~~~

Later, as Tony was helping his mother put away groceries, he nonchalantly brought up his encounter with the beauty across the street.

"I can't imagine how she got that trunk as far as the lawn. She did say she packed the books after she put the trunk in her car. She probably didn't realize how much they'd weigh." Wanting to talk about Ellen, he rambled on. "Not that she seemed helpless."

13

"That's nice dear," his mother said. Half listening, she handed him canned goods to place on the top shelf of the pantry. "My, my, those girls move in and out a lot. I wish Mr. Blackburn would just sell that house to some nice stable couple. I don't know how Lois stands it. Last night they played those awful Elvis Presley records until well after midnight and that Jerry Lee Lewis," she huffed. "There ought to be a law. Why, heaven only knows what goes on over there! If I inquire, Lois just changes the subject. I mean, it's not like I pry."

Three hours earlier Tony would have thought his mother knew what she was talking about and agreed, but after meeting Ellen he was just irritated. "I believe the girl who played the loud music moved out. That's what Abby said anyway," he mumbled.

"Abby, who's Abby?" she questioned with little interest.

"I think I'll take Jen to the park," he said abruptly.

"Okay dear, let's eat around seven."

Tony hurried Jenny into her coat.

"Don't forget her mittens. It's still cool out," she reminded him.

"I know," he snapped back.

"Tony? Is anything wrong?"

"No, no, everything's fine, Mom."

14

He tried to ignore her quizzical look as he rushed Jen out the door. *Yes, probably. I probably should stop thinking about the tall beauty across the street.*

Chapter Three

Lois Collins took a gulp of coffee, scalding her mouth, and winced. Sitting the paper cup on her desk, she swore softly. Judy Sands heard her swear and raised her eyebrows in disapproval.

The three secretaries shared a common room, with their desks sitting five feet apart. Lois was secretary to the senior Mr. Tate. Judy Sands and Mary Catherine Larson were secretaries to the two sons.

Mary Catherine, secretary to the youngest Tate, sat blowing her nose repeatedly while Lois and Judy exchanged irritated glances over her head.

"Do you have a cold or allergies?" Lois asked impatiently. It infuriated her when people came to work spreading germs to everyone within breathing distance.

Sniffling, she responded, "I'm okay," and then pushed her chair back, stood, and ran from the room.

Lois looked at Judy, "What? I only asked if she had a cold?"

Rolling her chair away from her desk, Lois followed Mary Catherine into the restroom and knocked on the stall door. "Are you okay Mary?"

Her sobs subsided long enough to answer a muffled, "Yes, I'm fine."

"No, you're not," Lois said sternly. "Come out of there this minute and tell me what's going on."

Opening the door slowly, Mary came out. "I'm sorry. I thought I could deal with this but, but..." Her tears started again.

"Wash your face and I'll get you some water."

Mary was drying her tear-splotched face on a paper towel when Lois returned with a cup full of water.

"Mark left us," Mary blurted out.

"What? When...how...why?"

"I picked up Jill from preschool yesterday, and when I got home, there was a note on the table. He said he was going back to his wife."

"Did you know?"

"No."

"His wife? I thought you were his wife?"

"I am. He went back to his ex-wife," Mary said and continued to cry.

"Well, you can't work like this. Go home. I'll cover for you. Do you want me to come by after work?"

"I'd appreciate it. I've only lived here a few months, and you and Judy are the only people I know."

Lois sighed heavily, "Listen, Mary, I'm divorced. It's not the end of the world. It only seems like it. Stay here. I'll get your purse and tell Mr. Tate you're sick."

"It's the truth."

"Yes, I know, I know," Lois said sighing.

Mary studied her reflection in the mirror over the restroom sink. *Why does this keep happening to me? How can I tell Lois I know all too well about divorce? Who would believe I'm only twenty-nine and this is my fourth failed marriage?*

In moments, Lois returned carrying Mary's coat and purse. "Here you are, dear. Are you sure you can drive?"

"I'll be okay, but what about the work?"

"Don't worry. It's not as if anyone's breaking down the door to see Brandon Tate. Here, write your address down, and I'll come by after work."

Mary Catherine scribbled her address, handed the paper back to Lois, and whispered, "Thank you."

"Go home, have a good cry, and get some rest. I'll come by later."

~~~

Stepping into the elevator, Mary couldn't decide if she was doing the right thing. She had thought coming to work would get her mind off things, but it hadn't. She tried to compose herself as the elevator door opened to the lobby. People were going about their business oblivious to her pain. A couple walked by in front of her holding hands and gazing into each other's eyes. They almost bumped into her, but hardly noticed.

Her mind reeled as she thought back to the start of her relationship with Mark. A mutual friend invited them to a party, but she'd paid little attention to him. He was short, shorter than her, and stocky, with piercing brown eyes and a nose too big for his face.

Later in the evening when everyone was dancing, she noticed him sitting alone, and she asked him to dance. Mark warmed to her kindness at once and was quick to confide that his wife had left him while he served in Vietnam. Freshly out of the service, he was still reeling from the 'Dear John' letter.

Mary could commiserate. Her third husband had recently walked out, leaving her with a toddler. Drawn together through suffering, he soon moved in with her. The union was inevitable. Her compassionate heart had compromised her virtue on more than one occasion. When Mark proposed, Mary quickly said yes. She wasn't madly in love

19

with him, but she reasoned that what they had was enough to build on.

Not long after their marriage, Mark decided to go to college, and Mary was full of encouragement. She was determined to make this marriage work, and if she had to support them while he went back to school, she was willing to make the sacrifice. Sadly, while he was supposedly studying at the library, he was having an affair with his first wife.

Once again, Mary Catherine was alone. Backing the car out of the office parking lot, she compared yesterday to today. How could so many things go wrong in just a few hours? She had no lofty ambitions, she only wanted to be loved, but her entire life had been a series of disappointments.

Hardly aware of what she was doing, she pulled her car into the parking lot of the liquor store. Walking in, she tried not to make eye contact with the man behind the counter. Greasy and unkempt, he made an insinuating remark. She paid for the bottle of gin and stuffed the change into her purse. *I don't care what he thinks. Somehow, I've got to have something to help me through this day.*

Chapter Four

"Joan!" Abby rushed into the house yelling and slammed the door behind her.

"Abigail, is it possible for you to enter a room without raising the roof?" Joan asked in disgust.

"Guess who just pulled into our driveway?" Abby asked undaunted.

"The president," Joan replied sarcastically. Paying little attention to Abby's exuberance, she sat thumbing her way through a magazine.

"That's close!" Abby squealed.

Joan gave her a blank stare.

"I was getting the mail, and he slowed down at our drive. I tried not to pay attention, and I hurried into the house, but…" She pointed toward the door, too excited to do anything but whisper, "It's Peter Ellington, as in the Ellingtons that own half of Cloverton."

Now she had Joan's interest. "Really?"

The two moved quickly to the window and peeked between the blinds.

"He's getting out of his car. What's he doing here?" Joan whispered. "He's so handsome. Are you sure it's him?"

"I don't know what he's doing here, but I'm sure it's him. I've seen his picture on the society page. Look at his car. Is that a Corvette?" Abby caught her breath and squeezed Joan's arm. "Look, he's coming up our walk!"

"Abby, stop it. You're acting like a silly schoolgirl."

"I am a schoolgirl, part-time anyway."

Turning, Joan whispered, "Maybe…"

Abby frowned, "Maybe what?"

"Katrina," Joan whispered. Passing a mirror, she fluffed up her hair and waited for the doorbell to ring. Trying to look surprised, she opened the door. "Yes?"

"I'm sorry to bother you, but I seem to be lost. Do you know where 215 Everest Street is?"

"This is 215 South Everest," Joan answered. "Who are you looking for?"

"I'm sorry, I can't seem to read my own writing," he laughed nervously. "Actually, as I look at this closer, I believe it is an N before Everest." He held the paper down so Joan could look at it with him. "Does that look like an N to you?"

"Yes, I believe it does," she said, giggling as she moved her face closer to his. "I'm afraid you're on the wrong side of town."

22

Offering his hand, he smiled warmly, "I'm Peter Ellington, and you are?"

"Joan, Joan Newel. Nice to meet you," she said shaking his hand.

Realizing Abby was standing in the doorway she said, "And this is Abigail MacDonald, one of my housemates." Peter nodded a hello. The silence was getting a little awkward, but Peter seemed in no hurry to leave.

"Well, maybe I'll see you around sometime," he said.

The two nodded, and everyone continued to smile. Peter started to walk away and then turned. The women remained standing in the doorway. He hesitated and then said, "Uh…I know we just met, but would you like to go for a drink or something?"

Joan swallowed hard as she strained to keep her excitement in check. "I think that would be nice."

Abby, over her shoulder agreed, "Yes that would be very nice."

Turning, Joan glared at her.

"For you and Joan, I mean. Not for me. I'm busy." Abby shook her head up and down and then back and forth laughing nervously.

"I have an appointment," he said looking at his watch, "but I'll be free in about an hour. Can I pick you up?"

"That would be great," Joan smiled.

23

As his Corvette pulled out of the drive, Joan waved. Abby, unaware of the dynamics, also waved.

Stomping into the house, Joan slammed the door. "What were you doing out there?"

"I thought he was talking to both of us. Besides, you have a date with John Elwood tonight."

"That's your problem, you think too much. Why would I keep a date with John Elwood If I could be with someone like Peter Ellington?"

"I-I-I guess I don't know."

"I-I-I guess *you* don't know," Joan mocked in a sing-song voice. "I've dreamed of meeting someone like him all of my life. Katrina promised me it would happen, and you nor anyone else is going to get in my way! Do you understand?"

Raising her eyebrows, Abby threw her hands in the air and watched as Joan marched down the hall. "I should have moved out with Bonnie," Abby whispered to herself.

Chapter Five

The sound of pounding was rousing Mary Catherine out of a deep sleep. Somewhere, someone was hitting something or someone. Halfway in a stupor, Mary Catherine mumbled her plea, "Please don't go. Oh please, please, I'll do anything."

Battling to escape the nightmare, she forced herself awake. In the last moments of the dream, she was pleading with Mark, but then his face morphed into the face of her father, and she was awake, and he was gone.

Forcing herself to sit up, she finally realized someone was banging on her front door. She glanced at the clock and groaned. "Six o'clock!" It was past time to pick up Jill and the daycare would fine her a quarter for every minute she was late.

"I'm coming," Mary hollered. Slipping on her shoes, she stumbled toward the door.

Lois and Judy walked in, and both seemed irritated. "We were worried sick about you," Lois stormed.

Eyeing the half-empty bottle of gin near the sofa, Judy sighed in disgust.

"I'm sorry, I was so sound asleep I didn't hear you."

Seeing how undone Mary was, Lois softened. "Are you okay?"

Embarrassed, Mary realized her eyes were probably bloodshot, her face puffy, and her hair a mess. She picked up her purse and hurried toward the door avoiding eye contact. "Yes, yes, but I have to get my daughter, Jill."

"I'll drive you," Lois volunteered, and then added, "I'm sorry we barged in on you like that. We were just so scared when you didn't answer the door."

Mary, overcome with shame, sensed the raw disapproval in Judy's countenance. Sitting in the front seat with Lois, Mary gave directions. "It's the daycare on Fifth Street."

"I think I know the one," Lois said. She studied Mary a moment before starting the car. "It's going to be okay," she whispered. "Why don't we take you and your little girl to dinner? It might help to keep your mind off things."

"That would be kind, but you don't have to."

"We insist," Judy called from the back seat.

"Turn left at this next light," Mary said.

"Yes, I know the one. We take Jennifer there," Judy volunteered. And then, remembering she should show some compassion, added, "Everything will be fine dear. We'll just tell them you had an emergency."

As they drove, and although it was completely off the subject, Judy managed to direct the conversation to the importance of church attendance and how having a strong commitment to a church body can make a tremendous difference in stabilizing your life. It was awkward, but she wanted to make sure Mary knew where she was coming from. Ignoring her, Lois droned on about the evils of men, her ex-husband in particular.

Arriving at the daycare, Mary Catherine jumped out of the car the second it stopped. She soon reappeared with three-year-old Jill in tow.

"These nice ladies are taking us to dinner," she explained to the child. "Maybe I should sit in the back with Jill," she whispered to Judy as she opened the back car door. Judy agreed and moved to the front.

Lois drove confidently with one hand on the steering wheel, the other holding a cigarette, which she waved about as she talked, filling the car with noxious fumes. Judy glared at her in disapproval and then rolled down the window. Mary drew Jill close to her side and tried to block out the chatter in the front seat.

Memories from her past flashed through Mary Catherine's mind, and they all seemed like yesterday. Her little sister Rose had been near Jill's age when her father left them. Her brother, Phillip, was an infant when her mother tried to kill herself and ended up in the psych ward.

At the time, Mary Catherine was only thirteen, but she hadn't allowed herself the grief that would have been natural. She knew little of what was happening, only that her siblings would live with her father and his new wife, and she would be shipped off to her paternal grandmother.

Lois interrupted her musing, "Is Italian okay?"

"Sure, we like spaghetti, don't we Jill?" She smiled down at the little girl, a miniature of herself.

Lois and Judy chattered nonstop throughout the meal and Mary began to tire. After an hour of continuous talking, the two asked Mary if she was ready to go home.

Startled by the question, Mary wondered if any place would ever feel like home again. Her last memory of a happy home was when she was seven years old. Back then she was Daddy's little princess. He took her fishing, teased her, and made her feel special. Going from man to man, she had searched for that special feeling, but it always ended in disaster.

Married at seventeen, she had high hopes of making a home for Phillip and Rose and had naively thought if she was married, perhaps she could gain custody of her siblings. Two months into the marriage, her husband lost his job and soon took his anger out on Mary Catherine by using her as a punching bag.

In financial desperation, she had married her second husband. He lied about his ability to take care of her, was an alcoholic, and considered anything in a skirt fair game. Her third husband gambled away every penny she made. Coming to her senses in less than a month, she left him. But then she met Mark, and once again she had dreams of a happy life, believing he was different, stable, and dependable.

As they pulled up in front of her house, she wanted the evening to be over. Suffering a raging headache from her previous indulgence, she only wanted to go to bed. Once inside, Lois suggested they stay for a while. Minutes into the conversation, Mary Catherine realized they both had an agenda. Judy wanted her to attend church on Sunday, while Lois wanted to give her advice, suggesting she sue Mark for every penny he had. After what seemed to be an eternity, the two said their goodbyes.

Hearing the car pull away, she heaved a sigh of relief, helped Jill into her pajamas, and tucked her into bed. Eyeing the half bottle of gin on the table, she willed herself to walk past, but then turned back and carried it into the bedroom.

Chapter Six

Returning home later than she anticipated, Judy said a quick goodbye to Lois, slid out of the car, and rushed up her driveway. The house was unusually dark, without a single light on, and she wondered where Tony and Jen could be.

Finding the door locked, her puzzlement was beginning to turn into fear when she heard Tony's familiar laughter. "Mom, I'm coming," he called to her from across the street. "Sorry about the lights." He rushed up to the door breathlessly, key in hand. Jennifer, riding on Tony's shoulders, squealed in delight.

"We played basketball with Ellen," Jen volunteered.

"In the dark? Who's Ellen?" Judy asked.

Tony unlocked the door, and his mom went through the house flipping on lights and trying not to be angry.

"I told you about her, Mom, remember? She moved in a while ago after Bonnie Bailey moved out."

Judy could feel her anger mounting, but she wasn't sure why.

"I vaguely remember," she said coolly. "Isn't it a little difficult to shoot baskets in the dark?"

Tony chose not to respond to the subtle insinuation that he was doing something wrong. "We only shot baskets until dark, and then Ellen suggested we eat supper with them, and since you and Lois were going to be eating out tonight, I just thought…"

"Them who?"

Seeing the look of disapproval on her face, he took a deep breath and tried to explain, "Ellen and her roommate Abby."

Blinking nervously Judy inquired, "Tony, what do you know about these girls? Do you think you should be getting involved?"

"Mom, it was basketball and chicken casserole, not exactly what I would call a romantic encounter."

Tony's voice was edgy, but Judy found herself unable to stop the interrogation.

"Well, I don't think these girls are a very good influence on Jennifer. From what I've heard about them from Lois, they are all pretty wild."

"Mom!" Tony stopped her in mid-sentence with a glance at Jennifer signaling her to stop.

Jenny looked from her father to her grandmother and then asked, "What's fluence, Daddy?"

"The word is influence, sweetheart, and we'll talk about it later. Right now, it's time for your bath."

Judy opened her mouth to speak and was stopped by Tony's firm, "Later, Mom," as he followed Jen back to her room.

They seldom disagreed, and Judy knew she was building a wall with her words. Sadly, her sense of righteous indignation would not allow her to back down.

Flipping on the kitchen light, she was surprised. The breakfast dishes were still on the table. Tony usually washed them before he left for work.

She gasped as worrisome thoughts bombarded her mind. *Maybe he went to Ellen's before work! Maybe this has been going on for a while. No, that can't be. The girl called Bonnie only moved out a few weeks ago.*

While running water in the sink, she wiped off the table and cleaned the stovetop. The bubbles were flying left and right as she plunged the dishes into the soapy water. Deep in thought, she didn't hear Tony come into the kitchen and jumped as he touched her elbow.

"Mom, we've got to talk." His voice was gentle, but his eyes were troubled. Motioning her to a kitchen chair, he sat down, but she remained standing, leaning against the counter.

"Come on Mom," he said cajoling her. "I'm sorry. I didn't mean to snap at you or leave you locked out in the dark. And about the messy kitchen, Tim called and needed a ride to work so I had to leave earlier than I planned. I know it wasn't very pleasant to come home to, I'm truly sorry."

Judy's heart melted. Sitting down, she rubbed her temples with her fingertips but said nothing, thinking, *I've already said too much.*

Tony sighed, "Okay, Mom, let's see, where do I begin?"

"Begin?" She caught her breath, fearful there might be more to the story than she wanted to know. "What are you talking about?"

He sighed, there was so much he wanted to say, and he could feel her resistance.

Judy looked intently into his eyes, afraid of what she would hear.

"Mom, Ellen's not like anyone I've ever known. She only moved in a short time ago, and I've scarcely talked to her, but I already feel…well… comfortable with her. It's hard to explain, but it seems as if I've known her all my life."

34

"And what do you know about her background? Is she a Christian...a believer?"

"I asked her if she had found a church since moving to our town. She laughed and looked a little mysterious."

Judy opened her mouth to speak, and Tony stilled her with a raised hand. "She told me she hadn't, but that she was trying to find a church and was praying about the right one. Then she told me that she attended church all of her life but never understood God's love until recently."

Judy could no longer contain herself. "And what in the world is that supposed to mean?"

"I'm not sure what she meant. When I asked her denominational background, she laughed and said that it wasn't really important. She said she had recently realized she was created to love God and that he had a plan for her life, and now more than anything, she is a seeker."

"Seeker? What kind of cult is that?"

"Mom, I know this may sound strange, but I feel like Ellen really knows God, knows Him in a way I want to know Him. She said everything in God's Kingdom starts and finishes with a relationship with Jesus and that she is trying to get to know Jesus and follow God in every area of her life."

"And you found this all out over basketball?" she asked sarcastically.

"No, it happened over dinner."

"Humph!" Judy said in disgust. Too angry to speak, she silently got up, walked to her bedroom, and closed the door.

Chapter Seven

Although Joan's first impulse was to seduce Peter and then control him through favors, her heart betrayed her. Within a month, she had fallen deeply in love and was willing to do whatever he wanted. He suggested she quit her job at the bank and come to work for him as his private secretary, and she eagerly accepted the offer.

The office chatter inferred Joan had skills besides her very capable office abilities, but Joan ignored the busybodies. After her last failed marriage, she bleached her hair white, lost fifteen pounds, and made up her mind to only marry for money.

She felt little remorse over the sudden dumping of John Elwood. John was a likely candidate before she met Peter. But John was only an electrician. He made a good living, but Peter could give her prestige as well as every material thing she had ever wanted.

It was noon of the first day on her new job when Peter peeked around the doorframe of her office and whispered her name. She looked up expectantly. "Hi beautiful, are you ready for lunch? One of the perks of being the boss' son is long lunches."

"And do I get paid for these long lunches?" she whispered back with a smile.

"Absolutely," he laughed. "And I know a little place beside the river that you will just love."

Joan gathered her things, and the two tiptoed out of the office side door, giggling like naughty children. The yellow convertible stood waiting. The sun was shining, and Peter was looking at her with adoration.

Joan had yearned for wealth and position all of her life, but Peter seemed to be offering her more than she had ever hoped for. His every action spoke of how much he cared, and the deep hole in Joan's heart was finally being filled.

The road to the river was winding and bumpy, and they laughed uproariously at the danger as they careened around corners at a high speed.

A tiny church on the top of a hill momentarily overshadowed her delight. Its steeple pointed toward the heavens like an accusing finger. Joan shuddered as memories of her father preaching fire and brimstone tried to attract her attention.

Peter watched her with a puzzled look. "What's wrong, Sugar? You look so serious."

"Oh, nothing," she said, leaning closer to him.

Trying to shake the shadow of her old life, she silently argued with her father. *I'm happy and you're not going to rob me.*

Peter's cheerful proclamation, "We're here!" interrupted her angry memories. She looked down at her clenched fists and willed herself to relax.

Getting out of the car she was surprised to see not a restaurant, but a beautiful little cottage tucked away in a cove of trees.

"Peter, I love it, but where are we?"

"It's my family's hunting lodge, but no one's here this time of year. I had a friend stock the refrigerator. Are you hungry?"

"Famished."

"We need to get to know each other. I thought we could take the afternoon off."

"But Peter," she laughed confused, "this is my first day on the job!"

"You can start tomorrow." His tone promised more than food and talk, and his hand on her back was warm and loving as he guided her into the cabin.

Although trembling with excitement from his touch, she couldn't stop thinking about Katrina Polworth. *Her readings are true. Everything Katrina promised is happening and happening faster than I could have ever imagined.*

As Peter pulled her close and covered her face and neck with kisses, her thoughts of Katrina faded into a blur, and yet it seemed as if Katrina was somehow with them.

Joan pulled away giggling. "We have all afternoon."

Giving her one last lingering kiss, he surrendered. "Yes, you're right, you're right," he apologized. "And I did promise you lunch." Popping the cork on a chilled bottle of champagne, he instructed her to look in the fridge. She brought out fresh fruit, two kinds of meat, and an assortment of cheese and crackers.

Setting the tray on the rustic coffee table, she sank into the comfort of the sofa. Petter filled her glass with champagne and made a toast. She blinked nervously and wondered if she had heard him correctly. It sounded as if he had said, "To us, for today and all of eternity!"

The assurance she felt at his toast was heady. She had scarcely known him a month, but this sounded very close to a marriage proposal. Closing her eyes, she leaned into his kiss, but she was not thinking of Peter but of Katrina. *Oh Katrina, why did I ever doubt you? Everything you promised is coming true.*

Chapter Eight

The little bell over the door of the bookstore rang out cheerfully. Not seeing anyone as she entered, Ellen called out, "Hello?"

"I'll be right with you," a voice spoke from behind a pile of boxes. Phoebe Brown, the owner of the bookstore, popped up from a mountain of cardboard. Recognizing her customer, her smile lit up the room. "Ellen! What a wonderful surprise!"

"Oh Phoebe, I hope I didn't come at a bad time, but I'm so excited I couldn't stay away." Looking around, Ellen frowned. "But you're really busy. Maybe I should come back later."

"Nonsense, I'm never too busy for you."

"I brought coffee and donuts. Can you take a break?"

"If you don't mind all the boxes," Phoebe laughed.

Ellen pulled a box down from the stack and made herself comfortable. Handing Phoebe a paper cup of coffee, she opened a bag of glazed donuts and pushed them toward her friend. "Before I forget, I'm so sorry I've missed Bible study the last two weeks. This is our busiest time of year, and I keep having deadlines."

Phoebe dismissed her apology with a wave of her hand, helped herself to a donut, and motioned for Ellen to continue.

"I don't know if I'll make it back this week either, but I just had to tell you."

Phoebe looked up with interest.

"Remember when I was complaining about my finances."

Phoebe nodded, "Yes, and you asked me to pray about it."

"Well, you'll never guess what happened. One of my co-workers invited me to live with her."

"So you are moving," Phoebe smiled. "That was certainly a quick answer."

"I know," Ellen laughed. "Actually, I've already moved! My co-worker, Abby, and two other women share a house. It's a beautiful home with four bedrooms in a much better neighborhood, and my rent has been cut in half."

Ellen reached for another donut. "But that's not all." She peeked shyly over her coffee cup. "I've met someone."

"Ah-ha, the plot thickens."

"I'm not saying anything will ever come of it. He lives across the street from my new place, and I kind of drafted him into helping me move my trunk."

Phoebe raised her eyebrows in question.

"He lives with his mother and three-year-old daughter. His wife died last year. I don't know the details…some kind of accident, I think. Anyway, he's volunteered to fix my car. Can you believe it? Three answers to prayer!"

"So, tell me a little more about this man who has you all a twitter," Phoebe teased.

Ellen blushed, "Actually, I don't think he knows what to think of me. We were having a conversation, and I told him that about a year ago I had a spiritual experience, and now following God has become the most important thing in my life. I figured if we were going to have any kind of relationship, I might as well get it out up front."

"Hmm," Phoebe said. "So what was his response?"

Ellen sighed, "I have to admit he looked confused, but I thought he would either be interested in learning more or he would write me off as a nut case and run."

"Is he a believer?"

"Well, he says he is. I mean, he goes to church and everything."

"Just one caution, don't go too fast."

"Yes, I know, but what if God put us together?"

Phoebe cocked her head and smiled in a teasing way, "A big if."

"I know, I know, and if it's not God's will, I don't want it, but it's just that…well…he's sooooo cute."

Phoebe just shook her head.

"He has blonde hair that he keeps brushing off of his forehead when he's nervous. He's tall and muscular and…"

"Oh dear, guard your heart, Ellen."

"I'll be careful. I don't want to mess up my life, and I also have another concern."

"Yes."

"It's not about him, it's about one of my new roommates. Her name is Joan, and honestly, I think she absolutely hates me."

Phoebe took a sip of coffee and frowned. "Hmmm."

"No, really, I'm not kidding! If I walk into a room, she walks out. I've tried to have a conversation, but she hasn't said ten words to me since I moved in. Abby says she's moody, but I think she's involved in something dark. Did I tell you about Lois?"

Ellen pushed the box of donuts toward Phoebe, but she resisted. "Lois?"

"Lois is the other woman in the house. She and I were talking last night, and she told me Joan asked her if she wanted to go with her to have her cards read. Evidently, Joan goes to a woman named Katrina. I can't remember the last name."

"Polworth?"

"What?"

"Katrina Polworth."

"You know her?"

"I know about her."

"What do you know about her?"

"Well, she is pretty well known in Logan County. Some people say she's heavily into witchcraft, or Satan worship, or something like that. If it's not witchcraft, it's certainly New Age. I've heard her referred to as a white witch, and I believe that sometimes even the Police Department calls on her for clues."

"What's a white witch?" Ellen frowned.

"White witches say they only use their psychic powers to help people."

"Does she think she gets her powers from God?"

"I don't know."

"Spooky."

"Ellen, I don't know how comfortable I am with you living with a witch."

Ellen laughed, "I don't think Joan's a witch. She just goes for readings."

"Still…"

"Don't worry. Abby thinks Joan will probably be moving in with her rich boyfriend before the end of the month."

"I hope that's true, but tell me more about your young man."

"Well, his name is Anthony Sands," Ellen blushed.

"Hmm."

"I was in the driveway shooting baskets when Tony pulled into his driveway across the street."

Phoebe nodded.

"He said, 'hey, that looks like fun. Mind if I join you?' Before I knew it, all three of us were shooting baskets."

"Abby?"

"No, his little girl, Jen. She's adorable," Ellen gushed.

"Tony would lift her over his head and tell her to shoot. She would just giggle and giggle."

"Sounds like he's a great dad."

"Oh, he is. Abby came out to tell me dinner was ready, and we asked Tony if he wanted to stay."

Phoebe nodded.

"Well, he was reluctant at first. Then he remembered his mom had called and said she was with friends for the evening and would be eating out, so he said 'sure.' I asked him to say grace, and he looked really surprised. He seemed

46

uncomfortable and said a memorized prayer, but at least he prayed."

"Go on."

"Then, out of the blue, Abby said to me, 'Tell me what you believe about God. I didn't know people still prayed before meals. I thought blessing your food was well, kind of a superstition.' She didn't seem critical, just curious. I told her I didn't know as much as I wanted to, but I'd recently found out that as I got to know Jesus, I was also getting to know God."

Phoebe nodded and encouraged her to continue.

"Then Abby asked how you get to know Jesus. So, I told her about your Bible study."

"What did Tony say about that?"

"Mostly he just listened." Ellen glanced at her watch, "Oh, I have to get back to work! Mrs. Musgrave will have a cow if I'm late."

Ellen stood and Phoebe hugged her.

"Maybe they'll come with you sometime."

"Mrs. Musgrave?"

"No, your new friends, Tony and Abby," Phoebe laughed.

"Yes, that's what I'm hoping."

As Ellen left the store, Phoebe whispered a silent prayer. *Please, Lord, she's so innocent. Don't let her get hurt.*

Chapter Nine

Mary Catherine paced back and forth across her living room. She often paced when she was nervous or upset. "How can I be almost seven months pregnant?" she whispered to herself. *I wanted to have Mark's baby, and now Mark is gone. Should I tell him? Would it bring him back? No, I can't look back. I have to go on. Somehow, I'll make it work. I've always made it work before. I don't want him to come back just because of the baby.* Mary touched her abdomen cautiously.

Jill, sleeping slumped over the arm of the overstuffed chair, looked like a bedraggled angel with one shoe on and one shoe off. Her light brown curls fell forward, hiding the side of her face.

Picking her up, Mary carried her to her room and gently dressed her for bed. Neither she nor Jill had been sleeping well since Mark left. Mary automatically fixed herself a drink, then thought of the baby, and poured it down the drain.

I'm sorry, little baby. I hope I haven't already harmed you. I didn't realize you were on the way.

48

What now, what now? Walking from window to window, Mary peered out into the darkness, feeling as if her future was as dark as this starless night. *God, are you up there?* she whispered. *Do you have any answers?*

Mary contemplated the invitation to go to church with Judy on Sunday, but something inside of her resisted. *God, am I so evil that I don't even want to go to church?*

Memories of attending church with her grandmother while her mother was in the mental institution filled her mind.

I enjoyed going to church at first, but then... Another memory flooded her thoughts. *The gossipers had a heyday once they discovered my mother was not only in a mental facility but was expecting a baby. A baby that was obviously conceived a year after my father had remarried.*

Pulling her bathrobe protectively about her, she made a decision. *No, I will not submit Jill to the sideways glances and whispered accusations that I went through. If they talked about my mother, wouldn't they talk about me in the same way?*

Sighing dejectedly, she decided to boil some water for tea. As she waited for the kettle to whistle, she considered her predicament and silently spoke her heart to her unborn child. *Oh, my sweet baby, what kind of life can I give you? You've certainly chosen an inopportune time to come into our lives. Who are you, baby? Are you a boy or a girl?*

A knock at the door filled her with a fleeting hope...*perhaps it was Mark!* She drew back the curtain slightly only to find it was Lois. Opening the door a few inches she asked, "Yes?"

"I thought you could use some company."

"Yes, yes, I'm sorry. Of course...come in."

"I know it's late. I was out getting gas in the car, and I saw your lights were on. How are you doing? I noticed you weren't at work this afternoon." She laughed nervously, "Well, that was obvious since your desk is right next to mine." She waited a moment and then continued. "Judy said you had a doctor's appointment. Is everything okay?"

Mary Catherine motioned for Lois to sit in the overstuffed chair, and she sat on the sofa across from her. Struggling for a moment, she decided to share her surprising news. "Yes, yes. I...ah...well, I guess you will know soon enough, and you may have already guessed. I'm going to have a baby." She blurted out the news and then started to cry.

"Is that such bad news?"

"Well, no, I guess not," Mary tried to smile through her tears. "I've suspected it for months, but I've never been regular and I...I...guess I just didn't want to face up to it. I wanted Mark's baby when we were married, but now…now…" Mary Catherine began to cry again.

"Oh, Mary, I'm so sorry. I know this must seem overwhelming."

"First I got the news about the baby, and then when I got home, the divorce papers were waiting for me in the mail."

Lois left the armchair and moved to the sofa beside Mary. She put her arm around Mary gingerly. Not usually a demonstrative person, she could feel Mary's pain and patted her awkwardly. From the kitchen, the tea kettle began to sing, and Mary welcomed the interruption. "Would you like some tea?" she called to Lois as she walked toward the kitchen.

"Yes, thanks, that would be nice. Do you have decaf?"

"Lemon Zest?"

"That's fine."

While sitting on the sofa, Lois mindlessly picked up the newspaper that was lying on the floor beside her chair. The headlines announced another child had been abducted; it was the third little girl to disappear in the last month. Lois shuddered and walked into the kitchen carrying the paper.

"What is this world coming to," she said as she sat down at the kitchen table and watched Mary brew the tea. Trying to get Mary's mind off herself, she began to discuss the most recent abduction.

51

"It says here the children just seem to disappear. No signs of a break-in or anything. Don't you find that strange?"

Mary, wrapped up in her own problems, paid little attention to Lois's commentary.

The two women sipped their tea silently for a moment, and then Lois said, "If you don't want the baby, I'm sure there are alternatives. That is, I heard about this doctor who…"

"No…no, that's not anything I could ever do."

Lois was silent, thinking back over her own life. *Not one of us knew what we could ever do until it seemed like it was the only answer,* she groaned inwardly.

Chapter Ten

She had stayed at Mary Catherine's house too long. Rushing home, she realized if she didn't do some laundry soon, she would be out of underwear. Busy sorting clothes to start washing, Lois murmured to herself, "I should have stayed home tonight. What good did I do Mary anyway?"

Hearing a car door slam, she grimaced. *Oh great, now what? I thought everyone was in bed but me. Who will be mad because I used the last of the hot water?* She looked at her watch. *One o'clock! I can't believe it. How will I ever get up in the morning?* Sighing, she listened for the sound of a key in the front door.

The click-clacking of high heels on the tile floor announced it was Joan. Lois braced herself. Joan always showered at night and would be furious if the hot water was gone.

Anticipating angry words, Lois turned slowly to face her accuser but then blinked in amazement. Joan was smiling, and her eyes were shining with a strange glimmer.

She stepped back as Joan stepped toward her.

"I'm so glad you're up!" Joan gushed.

Blinking and speechless, Lois tried to determine what Joan could mean.

"Oh, Lois, I'm so excited. I had to tell someone. I've spent all afternoon and evening with Peter…and now…now he wants me to move in with him! Can you believe it? Can you believe how fast this is going? It looks like I'll soon be Mrs. Peter Ellington! Today he told me he loves me!" she said breathlessly. "He said it was love at first sight, and he wants to be with me throughout eternity!"

"That's amazing. I've read in the paper that he's the most eligible man in the state. He's never been married, you know. It's a good thing that he's so open-minded."

"Open-minded?" Joan looked confused.

"About your previous marriages. Sometimes…I mean…well, evidently it doesn't matter to him."

The glee in Joan's eyes quickly turned to anger. "Why can't you just be happy for me? Are you jealous of my good fortune like the other two idiots who live here?"

"Well, no…," Lois tried to keep her voice calm. I just think honesty is the best policy, especially when you've so much at stake…I mean he's practically as famous as…as, well, you know, as a movie star. Surely you know there will be all kinds of gossip about his marriage."

Joan retaliated with a few choice swear words.

"I'm sorry Joan, It's just that…"

"It's not bad enough we've let that religious Ellen move in. Now I've got you to put up with too?"

Turning, she click-clacked back down the hall and slammed her bedroom door.

Lois turned to the pile of sorted clothes behind her and began to scoop them back into the clothes basket. *Maybe honesty isn't the best policy,* she reasoned. *It sure didn't help me much. Actually, honesty broke up my marriage. If I hadn't told Max about my affair with Byron, I would probably still be married. Because of honesty, I lost both of them.*

Sighing once more, she decided to further her apology. Tiptoeing down the hall, she knocked softly on Joan's bedroom door. At first, there was no answer, and then, "What do you want?"

"Joan, it's me. Can I come in?"

"The door's unlocked."

She entered the room and looked around. Everything was in perfect order. Joan sat on the bed removing her nail polish.

"I'm sorry, Joan. That was a stupid thing to say and…well, I agree…honesty is not always the best policy. Sometimes it's just plain dumb."

This surprising confession invoked a laugh from Joan, and Lois joined in. Joan's joyful countenance returned as she patted the bed. "Sit here and I'll tell you about my unbelievable day?"

Lois nodded, glad to be back in Joan's good graces and sat on the edge of the bed.

"Well, first of all, I've got to tell you about Katrina Polworth. Do you believe in the supernatural?"

"Well…, I don't know." She didn't want to risk Joan's anger again, but she certainly didn't believe in ghosts or spirits.

"Before you answer, let me tell you that I used to be just like you."

Lois stared at her round-eyed.

"Really, it's true! But then I started going to this woman for advice. Her name's Katrina and she's amazing. She told me that there is a power in the Universe that all of us can tap into. There are actual invisible beings all around us all of the time, and they want to help us. At first, I only went out of curiosity, but listen, you won't believe this! Katrina told me there's a spiritual wisdom from the beginning of the ages. It actually goes back to before time began and it's been passed down from generation to generation. Remember the Bible story about Adam and Eve? Remember how the snake told Eve she could know the difference between good and evil?"

"I wasn't raised in the church, but everyone knows the apple story. I never could understand how eating a piece of fruit would make God mad. Actually, the whole thing seems to be a bunch of silly myths."

Joan's eyes were shining with excitement. "Exactly, this is what I'm talking about! Katrina says Lucifer is the real god of this world. She says it's kind of like aliens from another world are helping us to find the truth! Isn't that fascinating? The real truth is that they aren't from another world. They're from another dimension! Since they've always been in this world, they know everything, and they are here to help us. We only need to invite them to live inside of us. Katrina calls them our spirit guides, and if we venerate them, they'll help us get everything we've ever wanted."

"Are you talking about flying saucers and all of that kind of thing?" Lois was trying not to show her disdain, but she was getting a little nervous.

Joan took her wide-eyed surprise as interest. "When I was growing up, my dad was a preacher, but we never had anything, and he was mean as a snake. I knew things had to be different. Now, I've finally found the truth." Joan jumped up, unable to contain her excitement. "It's all so simple. Don't you see? If Lucifer is the *God* of this world…and if he does control our destiny, don't you want to be on

57

his side? Katrina told me the serpent in the garden was not evil at all. In fact, he was a beautiful dragon and a liberator. He and the one that Christians call God have been in a war to rule this planet since before time. Isn't that exciting? The more we surrender our lives to the spirits, the more power we can have over the things of this world.

"But why can't we see them?"

"It's hard to explain, but Katrina said they had bodies, but they lost their bodies in the terrible flood."

Lois looked confused.

"You know the flood that God sent to destroy them. Now they are merely spirits, but they are looking for bodies to inhabit. You see, they can only operate on this plane when they have bodies to work through. When we surrender our bodies to them, we become one with them!"

Lois felt a shiver run down her spine. She'd only gone to church twice in her entire life, both times when she'd spent the night with a girlfriend. Even so, all of this sounded more than a bit creepy. She thought of the evening she'd spent with Mary Catherine and began to question everything she had ever heard about religion. *But what if this stuff is for real, Mary could sure use some power in her life. Still, it feels a bit crazy..., but maybe it's just because I don't understand it. This power certainly seems to be working for Joan.*

"Lois, do you want to go with me to see Katrina? I'm going tomorrow afternoon, and I could pick you up after work. Maybe your life is about to change for the better too."

Lois started to hesitate and then changed her mind. "Oh, what could it hurt?" she laughed nervously. "Maybe this is the answer I've been looking for." The two women suddenly became serious as they each imagined the endless possibilities of having anything they could ever dream of.

Chapter Eleven

A cheery fire crackled in the fireplace as an unusually cold April wind whistled around the house. Tony pulled his daughter close as he read the newspaper. His mother sat on the sofa to his left hemming a pair of Jen's slacks.

"She's so petite," she said, smiling at her work. "I think she'll always be small like her mother."

Tony looked up, troubled.

Jen squirmed away from him, jumped off his lap, picked up a doll, and began to play at his feet.

"Mom, are you following these stories in the newspaper?"

Judy looked up.

"About the disappearing children?"

"Yes, it's terrible, isn't it?" she clipped a thread and continued to sew.

Tony got up slowly and began going from room to room checking the locks on every window. Walking back into the living room he stood by the fireplace. "Mom, can you keep Jen tomorrow night? I'd like to go to a Bible study with Ellen."

He poked at the fire with a fire iron as if he'd made a casual remark, but her silence forced him to turn. She sat there, needle in hand, completely still.

"Mom, did you hear what I said?"

"I heard you," she said and concentrated on threading her needle.

He waited for her to drop the bomb of disapproval, but she remained silent. He was getting the picture. She would make him feel guilty by refusing to talk about it.

"I know our church frowns on fraternizing with other denominations, but I've been questioning that lately. Is that a commandment? If so, I haven't found it anywhere in the Bible. Don't many denominations agree with us on the important things? Think of it, Mom, do you believe we will all have separate areas of worship in heaven? Ellen says the Bible study she goes to has a lot of Christians from different denominations in attendance."

His mother caught her breath, trying to quote the appropriate Bible verse. "Come out from among them…," she said in a quivering voice. She knew there was something like that in the Bible, and it was the only thing she could think of.

He continued as if she hadn't said a word.

She looked like he'd punched her, but he continued, "I've started reading my Bible again. I used to read it when I was a little boy, but truthfully, as an adult, I've lost what little faith I had. It just didn't seem like the sermons Pastor Wind preached were relevant to my life."

Watching him as one would a madman, she drew back into the corner of the sofa and remained motionless.

Tony continued pacing in front of the fireplace, staring at the carpet as he walked. "Last year, when the accident happened," he hesitated, choosing his words carefully, aware that Jennifer was also listening to every word. He lowered his voice as if speaking in a quieter tone would soften the blows of his words.

"Last year when I thought God was somehow responsible for taking away the joy of my life, I questioned everything. If this was the way God was, I didn't want anything to do with Him."

His mother started to speak, but he interrupted. "I know, I know, the grief counselor said anger is a natural part of the grieving process, even anger at God, but Mom…" He knelt beside her and looked into her eyes. "I don't believe God wanted us to suffer this loss. Since I've been talking to Ellen, I've come to realize how much God loves me, how much he loves you and Jennifer. I understand things about God I never knew before.

We have a real enemy. And he wants to destroy us. Ellen says these things that happen…like Carol's death, happen because we live in a fallen world…a world where Satan is constantly trying to bring things into our lives to make us doubt God's love. She says in the Bible it says Satan is the God of this world and the evil that happens is because of him…not God."

"But Tony…Tony…Tony. The Devil can't be everywhere. That's ridiculous."

"Mom, surely you remember about the fallen angels…the angels that followed the Devil…you know…Demons?"

Judy could take no more. Her tone was even, but her words clipped. "Of course I do. I suppose Ellen with her degree in fashion design or home economics or whatever…knows more about God than Pastor Wind!"

"Yes, in some ways, I believe she does," he answered softly. "Actually, her degree is in education, but she has always dreamed of designing wedding gowns, and she moved here to fulfill that dream."

"Oh, Tony! Where have I gone wrong?" She covered her face with both hands.

The question was rhetorical, but he answered it anyway. "Mom, you didn't go wrong. You taught me what you knew, took me where you thought best, and carried on the traditions that have been in our family for generations, but I want more than tradition. I want more for me, and I also want more for you and Jen. There is a spiritual war going on all around us...evil against good, good against evil. I've just let things happen to me. I've been a spectator, not realizing that I have the authority to come against these entities through the sacrifice of Jesus Christ. I want to *know* that I belong to Jesus! That I'm on God's side. I want to fight this evil...like...like..." He picked up the newspaper and pointed to the headlines, "Like that! I want to pray, have faith, and see things changed. I want to pray and to know that my prayers make a difference!"

"But how can you do anything to stop what some monster is doing?"

"Ellen says this kind of terrible thing will only be stopped by prayer! Mom, do you realize I'm an adult man and I don't even know how to pray? I've gone to church all of my life and the only way I know to pray is to say what I've memorized. To speak by rote words that came out of someone else's heart."

"Tony there is nothing wrong with praying memorized prayers. Why, I can't tell you the many times that just saying the Lord's Prayer aloud has helped me."

"Okay, Mom," he sighed, dropping his head. "I know memorized prayer has its place and it can be prayed very effectively when it is prayed from your heart, but that's not what I'm talking about. I'm talking about all of us Christians who go to church Sunday after Sunday just because we always have. We don't even realize there's a spiritual war going on! Bad things happen to us, and we just think, 'Well that's life.' We sit in the pews, sing the songs, and go home satisfied, but while we are complacently going about our lives, the Devil is wreaking havoc, gaining ground not only with us but with the people around us, and we are calling these things *acts of God*!"

"Tony, I know there's a Devil, I just don't want to think about him."

"I don't want to think about him either, Mom. I just want to partner with God and fight Evil."

She stared at him as if he had lost his mind, as if he were about to go out and buy a Superman costume and jump off a building.

He could almost see Ellen shaking her head and saying, "Battles are won by prayer, Tony, not arguments."

"Tony, I don't understand what you're trying to say?"

"Just that I love you, Mom, but I am a grown man, and I am on a spiritual quest. If I decide God is prompting me to attend another church, I don't want us to get into a battle."

She drew in her breath and covered her mouth with both hands.

"I'm not saying I will, but if I do, we can't be arguing about this all the time."

He'd gone too far. This was more than she could take. Her eyes brimmed with tears of frustration. Trying to keep her tone even she said, "Tony our family has gone to the same church for five generations!"

He acted as if he hadn't heard. "Mom, there's something else I need you to know. I want to pursue a relationship with Ellen, and I want your blessing."

Her mind was reeling. *I knew it!* She thought. *That woman has him mesmerized. This is not about religion; this is about lust!* She hesitated a moment, trying to gather her thoughts. If Jen had not been sitting there, she knew she would have given him a piece of her mind. *How dare he try to make me think he's on a spiritual quest when this whole thing is about that woman across the street in her short shorts.*

"Mom, I want you to meet Ellen. She's mentioned having us over for a cookout when the weather warms."

Jen, hearing Ellen's name, looked up and smiled.

"Ellen's my new friend, huh Daddy?"

Judy groaned inwardly. "I don't suppose you would consider speaking with Pastor Wind about this," she asked.

"No, I know you have to do what's in your heart to do, but I would appreciate it if you didn't talk to him either. Please Mom, just meet her first."

Judy nodded mutely, but she had already made up her mind. That woman would never be a part of her family…ever!

Chapter Twelve

Ellen opened the window and let the curtains flutter in the wind. The day promised to be warm and beautiful. She sang to herself as she began to peel potatoes for the potato salad and smiled across the table at Lois, who was busy forming ground beef into patties. The whirr of the mixer made conversation next to impossible as Abby beat egg whites for an angel food cake.

"It's so nice of you to help me with this cookout," Ellen hollered over the noise.

Lois saw Ellen's lips move but had no idea what she was talking about. "What?" she hollered back.

"I said…"

Suddenly the noise from the mixer stopped.

"What are you two yelling about?" Abby asked innocently.

Lois and Ellen laughed. "I was just saying how much I appreciate your help. I'm kind of nervous about meeting Tony's mother."

"You mean Judy? She's stuffy, but not scary," Lois remarked. "Before I forget, thank you for inviting Mary Catherine. I've wanted you to meet her, and I think her little girl is near the age of Tony's Jen."

"Yes, Tony mentioned they've met. Mary Catherine said Judy took them to church last Sunday."

Lois stood, "Well, the patties are ready. Do you want me to start the baked beans?"

"Oh dear," Ellen blinked nervously. "Do you think they can be in the oven with the cake?"

"Not my angel food cake!" Abby said protectively.

"Okay, maybe we should forget about the beans. Lois, do you want to help me move the picnic table out of the garage?"

"Sure."

Opening the garage door, the two stared at the table. "I forgot how big it was," Ellen sighed. "Maybe we should wait for Tony."

"Aww, come on, we can do it." Lois smiled and started toward one end of the table. "But maybe we should wait," Lois grinned. "You sure made the right move the last time he helped you carry something heavy. Judy tells me you two are spending a lot of time together."

Ellen could feel her face burning as she placed her hands on the opposite end of the table.

"Aha! I thought so," Lois teased. "And you thought you could pull this off as a friendly neighborhood get-together."

"This looks like a good place," Ellen said, steering Lois to an area under a big tree. "This will give us some shade."

"Are we trying to change the subject?" Lois teased.

"I admit I'm attracted to Tony, but right now we're just friends. I'm praying about continuing the relationship."

"Whoa!" Lois laughed. "Please don't tell me you pray about who you should date. I don't know who's worse, you running everything by God for His approval or Joan and Katrina conjuring up Joan's prosperous future."

"What are you talking about?"

"You know, Joan and Katrina?"

"I'm not sure I know what you mean?"

"Well, she kept saying what a spiritual experience she had with Katrina, and I'm a little embarrassed to admit it, but…I went for a reading last week."

"You what!" Ellen gasped.

"It's no big deal. To tell you the truth, I was a little frightened at first, but Katrina wasn't spooky at all. She looks like a regular person, no crystal ball or anything," she laughed. "And she's remarkable. She told me that next week she will get

70

me in touch with my spirit guide. I have to admit that's a little scary, but Joan told me that everything Katrina told her in the past, has already come true. Not only can she see into the future, but she can hold your hand and tell you things about your past. It's a little unnerving at first, but wow she is amazing! I've been thinking, maybe I'll ask Mary Catherine to go with me next time. I think she could use some encouragement, and besides, it's fun and it's not very expensive. You know… you would spend that much on a show or a dinner. You should come with us sometime."

Ellen tried to keep her composure while praying silently. *God, what do I say? This is no time to get into a discussion on the pros and cons of fortune-telling. I want to show these people love, not judgment, and I certainly don't want to get into a heated debate about religion.*

Lois took Ellen's silence for interest. "I know…isn't it exciting?"

"Well, it's interesting," Ellen smiled. "I'm on a spiritual journey myself."

Lois looked surprised. "Really? So, you'll go with us?"

"Well, probably not," Ellen smiled. "But I would like to talk about it sometime."

Back inside, Ellen wondered how she could discreetly telephone Phoebe and ask her for prayer.

Please, God, I need backup. Please have someone pray for me. I feel like I'm in way over my head.

Several miles across town, Phoebe suddenly remembered Ellen had asked for prayer. She started to go for the phone but changed her mind and instead quietly slipped into her bedroom, went to her knees, and prayed for Ellen to have wisdom and peace.

Chapter Thirteen

Katrina Polworth meditated before a flickering candle, praying to her spirit guide, Areone. He had been the first spirit to come to her the night her father raped her and then beat her for seducing him. She was only ten years old. Areone had appeared at the foot of her bed and told her he had come on a mission from another world to help her.

This was the beginning. She readily agreed to do whatever he asked, if only he would rescue her. He said he only wanted her obedience, and if she obeyed him, she would see every dream come true. As promised, he gave her the power to know things, things that other people found amazing. She was too young to understand, but this she knew…if anyone or anything could help her, she would do whatever they asked.

Katrina's father had been a Satanist from the time he was a young man. The night she pledged herself to Areone, her father shot himself. She heard the sound of a gunshot and her mother's screams, and she knew that somehow Areone had set her free.

Over the years, many spirits spoke to Katrina. They told her that they were the spirits of her ancestors, and it was easy to believe them as they knew things and revealed things that later proved to be valid information. They told her she was loved by those who were born and died before her, and that she was chosen. She revered them as they demanded, not knowing her father had dedicated her to Lucifer before she was born.

As an adult, Katrina learned how to manipulate the police department. They often came to her for help in solving crimes. She could feel Areone was pleased, and she promised him her soul for political power. Her obedience to the spirits became an obsession. They told her what political gatherings to attend and gave her the ability to look beautiful in the eyes of the men she wanted to seduce. As she gave herself to these men, her powers increased, and she made sure she documented each affair so that she could use the information to barter with them when necessary.

The doorbell rang, and Katrina stood and waited for the second ring before answering. The tall young man standing on the porch was in his late twenties. He was a handsome man, blonde with piercing gray eyes, and was dressed in a navy blue policeman's uniform.

"Sergeant Grant, what a nice surprise! You'll be happy to know we've changed the location of our meeting as you suggested. The room under Peter's farmhouse is finally finished. If you're not busy this afternoon, perhaps I could show it to you. It's really quite remarkable."

"Sorry, I'm tied up all afternoon."

She caressed his arm with her fingertips, leaned into him seductively, and whispered, "Perhaps another time."

He sighed and she took it as regret.

Blinking nervously, he gulped, but finally came to the point. "I came here to warn you that my chief suspects you of having something to do with the disappearance of those little girls. If you're involved in child trafficking, I won't be a part of it. Drugs and prostitution are one thing but not…"

She interrupted him, and for a moment her eyes flamed. "I told you our group has nothing to do with that. And what right do you have to question me? You've been well paid to look the other way Sargent Grant, and if you turn on me, you'll soon see your face smeared all over the front page. Believe me, it won't be pretty. We are in a war and the Luciferians will soon have world dominion. You know of our power. You don't want to be on the wrong side." She laughed a strange guttural laugh. "We already have our people in every level of government. We are capturing the media, and it won't be long before we'll convince the multitudes to follow us."

She watched him carefully for a reaction. His commitment to ignoring her sexual flirtations made her uncomfortable, and she wasn't sure she could trust him.

Feeling her misgiving, he nodded in agreement and listened as if in rapt attention to the monologue he'd heard more times than he cared to remember.

"Time is short, but many of us have become one with the Nephilim. Our people are everywhere, and it's so simple!" She wet her lips seductively and leaned against him. "Wait until we give everyone the scientific proof that they are from another planet and were placed here to help us. They'll easily surrender once they realize we're the ones with the power."

He listened patiently, but when she stopped for a breath, he jumped in. "So far, I've been able to convince the captain of your innocence, but…"

She searched his face eagerly, "But you have?"

"Yes, for now."

She frowned, sensing something was wrong. "I hope you realize that you're part of this spiritual battle. If you betray us, you may find those you love most have fallen into unfortunate circumstances."

Once again, he blinked nervously but she didn't seem to notice.

"There is a woman who has been coming here for readings for over a year. Later today, she'll be bringing her fiancé. She thinks he will be coming for his first reading. After this, I believe she'll be ready for the next step of her indoctrination."

Changing the subject, he cleared his throat and said, "I just want to clarify that you aren't in any way responsible for the child they found in the park. The coroner said this little girl had Satanic symbols carved on her abdomen and…"

"Sooo," she screamed, "what has that to do with me? There is more than one coven in this town."

"And you give me your word that you've had nothing to do with the disappearance of these children?"

She laughed and was about to speak when the telephone rang. Larry whispered, "I have to go." And quickly slipped away.

Chapter Fourteen

Jennifer twisted and turned excitedly as Tony tried to tie ribbons in her hair.

"Can you stand still?"

"Yes, Daddy," she said but was soon dancing as Tony's large hands fumbled with the tiny hair bows.

"Does Ellen like me, Daddy?"

"Yes, I believe Ellen likes you very much."

"And you, too. Ellen likes you very much too, huh Daddy?"

"Yes, I believe Ellen likes me very much too." Tony laughed light-heartedly at his tiny daughter's intuitiveness.

Judy appeared in the doorway just in time to hear the last comment, and Tony was well aware of her disapproval.

"Well, it's almost noon. I guess we should head over," he said light-heartedly.

"Look, Grandma." Jennifer twirled to show off her red poke-a-dot dress. "See, Daddy found poky-dot hair bows to match my dress."

"Polka-dot," Tony corrected.

Placing his arm around his mother's narrow shoulders, he gave her a loving squeeze. "Smile, Mom. It's a cookout, not a funeral."

"Come out from among them and be ye separate!" Judy once again quoted the Bible verse she often used when she didn't approve of someone's lifestyle.

"Mom, the Bible also says we are to be the salt of the earth."

"I don't see how that applies."

Tony sighed, refusing to get into an argument that would only make things worse. Instead, he changed the subject. "Oh look, Mary Catherine and Jill are here."

Jen bolted for the door in excitement. "Wait for us!" Tony warned. "Don't cross the street until we get there."

Judy continued to glare at Tony as he tried to cajole her into a better frame of mind.

"Mom, you were so happy last Sunday when Jill and Mary Catherine went to church with us. And it was so kind of you to invite them for lunch afterward. Can't you just be as happy in the same way now?"

"I was happy because we were going about this thing in the right way. I believe in pulling them into my world, not going where they are."

"Mom, can we just lay down our judgments and be kind? It's not as if we are doing something illegal or even immoral. It's just a neighborhood picnic."

"I want you to know, I'm doing this for you, but I don't in any way believe it's right."

Jennifer stood on the curb, waving excitedly at Jill across the street. "Come on, Grandma," she squealed in excitement, "my friend is here."

Tony gave his mother a cockeyed smile and they crossed the road.

~~~

The afternoon was spent playing croquet and eating until they were stuffed.

Purposely disregarding Ellen, Judy directed most of her conversation toward Lois or Mary Catherine. She ignored Abby as if she was invisible, placing her in the same category as Ellen. Tony noticed that Mary Catherine got very nervous every time his mother mentioned the church service last Sunday, and he wondered what was going on in her head. Ellen was her delightful self, totally uninhibited by the rejection Judy purposely aimed in her direction.

Abby followed Ellen into the kitchen to get more ice for the drinks. "Have we done something to make Judy mad?"

Ellen smiled and asked in sarcastic innocence, "Why would you ask that?"

"Wow, she's like a momma bear with her cubs. What does she think you're going to do to Jen and Tony?"

Ellen shrugged her shoulders and sighed. "I thought she didn't like me because she didn't know me, but now I see God's going to have to do a miracle. I can certainly see that she doesn't want me to continue dating Tony." She slowly shook her head, sighed heavily, and said, "Please, God, how do I handle this?"

"Ellen, I can't believe you." Abby giggled in a teasing manner. "Do you pray about everything...I mean things like, well, relationships and stuff? I thought you religious folks just prayed for people to go to heaven or ,ah, to get well when they're sick."

Ellen's sense of humor quickly returned. "I don't know what other Christians pray about, but I pray about everything, especially relationships!"

"And do you truly think it helps? Maybe you should stop praying. I think she's getting worse."

Ellen sighed and laughed softly. "I've learned that things aren't always as they appear. Sometimes I think things are going badly and all of a sudden God turns them around."

"You mean like that old saying, lemonade out of lemons?"

81

"Something like that, only better. That reminds me, will you get more lemonade out of the fridge? I think we're almost out. There's a verse in the Bible that promises us that when we want what God wants in our life, he makes everything work out for our good."

Abby looked thoughtful for a moment and then asked, "Well, doesn't God want good for everybody? I mean, if He knows what we want, I don't understand why He doesn't just give it to us. Why…why do you have to pray about everything all the time?"

"For one thing, God's given us free will. He doesn't interfere in our life unless we invite Him in. Do you know how it is when someone ignores you, how hard it is to talk to them?"

Abby nodded thoughtfully.

"Well, actually it's kind of the same way with God."

"Wait a minute, are you trying to tell me that not only do you speak to God, but He talks to you?"

Ellen smiled, "It's not an audible voice, but yes, I do have a sense of what He wants. I guess we better get back outside. If you're interested, maybe we can talk about this later."

Abby's eyebrows were knit in concentration as the two made their way back to the others. "I didn't know I was interested, but I guess I am. To tell you the truth, I thought you were kind of…strange…but, it's a nice kind of strange," she said, smiling at Ellen.

"Back to the battleground," Ellen said and smiled back.

"Just one more question," Abby whispered as they were going out the door. "Isn't Judy a Christian too? I'm confused. Aren't you all on the same team?"

Ellen raised her eyebrows, "Supposedly," she giggled.

Chapter Fifteen

Mary Catherine snuggled under the covers and listened to the thunder, thankful the rain had held off until dark. The picnic was far more fun than she had expected. *It was a relief to get my mind off my problems for a while. It was kind of Lois to invite us to the cookout. Jill certainly had a good time playing with Jen*, she mused.

The wind picked up and began to blow so hard, the windows rattled. Mary slipped out of bed quietly, checked on Jill, and pulled the covers up around her daughter's ears. She sighed, relieved Jill was sleeping through the storm.

Wide awake now, Mary began recounting the day's activities. *Judy was unusually snappy and moody, buy Lois' housemates seemed nice.* Mary sighed again, *at least it was something to do.*

Walking from room to room, she checked the windows. Everything was fine. They were all closed and locked. She flipped on the light in the kitchen and decided some toast and milk might help her sleep. The newspaper lay on the kitchen table where she'd left it this morning, unread. The bold print of the headlines shouted the news.

MISSING CHILD FOUND IN PARK

Fully awake, Mary read the paper with trembling hands. A toddler was found by joggers in the park only a few blocks from her home. They'd passed the child thinking it was a large, discarded doll. Circling back, they came closer, realized it was a child, and called the police.

Mary Catherine dropped the paper, shivering from head to toe. Was it too late to call Lois? She glanced at the clock above the stove and decided to risk it. Her fingers were shaking as she dialed the numbers. A sleepy hello answered her call.

"Lois?"

"No, this is Ellen."

"Oh, Ellen, I'm so sorry to wake you. I know it's after eleven. I thought maybe Lois was up. This is Mary Catherine."

"I think Lois is still out with Joan and Peter. Can I help?"

Mary hesitated, "I...I...I guess I'm just afraid. Did you read the paper today?"

"No, I didn't. With all the confusion of three cooks in the kitchen, I didn't have time."

"They found one of the missing children. A little girl."

Wide awake, Ellen sat up in bed and turned on her bedside lamp. "Alive?"

"No…they said it must have been a ritualistic murder. What does that mean?"

"Maybe a satanic ritual? I don't know, but it's hard to believe anything like that could happen in our sleepy little town."

Both women were silent for a minute.

"They found her in the park on Elk Street. That's just a few blocks from here. I take Jill there to play on the swings," Mary's voice broke. "I guess she was partially buried in a shallow grave. The paper said the recent rainstorms were responsible for…"

Ellen could tell Mary was trying not to cry.

"Mary, do you want me to come over?"

"That's very kind of you, but it's storming something awful, and I couldn't ask you to come. I've just been so emotional lately. I suppose it's the hormones, you know with the baby and all. I'm just so weepy."

"Give me your address. I'll be there as soon as I throw on some clothes."

Ellen pulled on jeans and a sweatshirt and searched to no avail for an umbrella in the bottom of the closet.

Father, I've been praying for Mary Catherine ever since Lois first told me about her problems.

Now it looks like you're allowing me to show her Your love. Please help me to say the right words.

The rain was coming down in sheets and lightning ripped across the sky as Ellen drove across town.

The porch light was on, and Mary opened the door before Ellen could get out of her car. Standing in the doorway, Ellen shook the rain off her jacket.

"Don't worry about that, please just come in. I'm usually not afraid of storms. It's just that what happened…I mean they found her so near and, this child was close in age to Jill."

"You don't have to explain."

"Now that you're here, I feel so silly. When I read the paper, I guess I just panicked. All the little girls that have been taken are around Jill's age or younger, but I kept hoping they would find them alive, and now…"

"Of course you're afraid. I don't think you're silly at all. Would it help if I prayed for you?"

Mary Catherine dropped her head. "Ah…well…," she sighed heavily, "I've been going to church with Judy."

"I see," Ellen said, feeling as if she had trespassed on Judy's property.

"At first, I told her no, but she was so persistent. It seemed easier to just give in. Last week after the service, she arranged for me to talk with her pastor. I guess she had talked to him

87

before. Somehow, she had given him the idea that I wanted to join her church. He said all I had to do was confess my sins and ask God to forgive me. They would baptize me, and I could join the church. He had me repeat a prayer and told me he would see me in the new convert's class next week and arrange for me to be baptized."

"How do you feel about this?"

"To tell you the truth, I know this sounds terrible, but I feel a little angry." She dropped her head and looked embarrassed. "Do you think I'm an awful person?"

"Of course not, but do you know why you felt that way?"

"I guess I don't feel like he really cared about me. I don't even know if God cares about me. I feel like I'm just going through the motions…like I'm just another notch on his belt."

Ellen made a face, "Sorry."

"I guess they're trying to help me." Mary sighed again. "But now I don't want to go back. Judy said I can't go by my feelings. She dropped her eyes. "Shouldn't I feel something? I don't even know if I believe in God. Sometimes I pray out of desperation. I wish I believed, but to be honest, I don't know what I believe."

Ellen prayed silently, *Lord now what? It isn't going to do her any good if I just do a repeat of Judy Sands or Pastor Wind.* "Mary, I'm sorry, sometimes we Christians show more zeal than love." Then she added softly, "I'm sure Judy and her pastor honestly want to help you. In their exuberance, maybe they've rushed you into something you're not sure of."

"I guess so...maybe," she said as she sighed another deep sigh. "To tell you the truth, Lois is kinder to me than Judy. Judy always makes me feel as if she has to sanitize me before she can have me for a friend. You know, kind of like when you find a stray puppy, and you give it a bath to kill the fleas before you bring it home."

Ellen smiled at the grimace on Mary's face.

"Don't feel bad, she looks at me the same way." The two women laughed together easily.

"I'd like to be your friend. I've just moved here myself, and I don't know many people either." Ellen said and then went on to explain how she'd been a school teacher, teaching Home Economics and living with her mom. She elaborated on her insecurities and her impossible boss and did impersonations of some of her crazy customers. Soon Mary was laughing lightheartedly. The time flew by, the rain stopped, the moon came from behind the clouds, and the danger seemed less menacing.

Looking at her watch, Ellen groaned, "I can't believe I've stayed so long. It's already one thirty. I

89

better get out of here so you can get some sleep. Do you think you'll be okay now?"

"I feel so much better. Thank you for coming. I haven't laughed like this in a long time."

"I do care about you and so do Judy and Lois. I hope you won't think I'm being too pushy, but I have this friend I met right after I moved here. I think you would like her. She has some amazing insights about life. I was confused about a lot of things, and she's really helped me. Her name is Phoebe Brown, and she runs the Christian bookstore on Adams Street. She and her husband have a really neat Bible study. No pressure, but do you think you might like to meet her sometime? I think you would like the Bible study too. Honestly, it's very casual and not intimidating at all."

Mary looked thoughtful for a moment. "Maybe. I'll think about it."

"I promise not to make any notches on my belt if you come," Ellen teased as she backed toward the door.

"Okay," Mary laughed, "if you can call me ahead of time so I can make plans to get a sitter, I'll give it a try."

Locking the door, Mary Catherine walked through the house. Nothing had changed, but somehow she felt lighter and more optimistic. *Maybe I do need to know more about Jesus,* she sighed. *Maybe He does have some answers for me.*

Chapter Sixteen

As Joan walked slowly through Katrina's well-tended flower garden, she was puzzled by the strange stone figurines featured in prominent places. She studied the large diamond ring on her finger in admiration as she contemplated her future. *This is really going to happen. It's not just a fantasy. The house, the position, everything I've ever dreamed of will soon be mine, but I should be happier. I should be ecstatic. What's wrong with me?*

Katrina had suggested Joan would enjoy the gardens while she gave Peter a private reading. Carrying the glass of fruit juice from Katrina, she sauntered among the flowerbeds. *It's such a beautiful, unseasonably warm afternoon*, she thought. *Why can't I just relax and enjoy the day?* Taking another big swallow of juice, she tried to determine its content. She couldn't decide if she liked it or not. It certainly had an unfamiliar flavor.

As she wandered among the flowers, she felt unusually drowsy. *This is strange,* she thought. *I never nap, here it is only two in the afternoon, and I can barely keep my eyes open.* Noticing a stone bench hidden in a secluded area of untrimmed bushes, she finished her drink and placed the glass beside the bench. *I'm so exhausted. Maybe if I just lie down on this bench for a while.*

"Joan? Joan?"

Is someone calling me? The trees above began to sway in the breeze, and the rustling of the leaves seemed to be softly whispering her name. Feeling as if she were floating, she left her body lying on the bench as if it were discarded clothing. Opening her eyes, she was not surprised to see herself sleeping far below on the stone bench. Floating higher and higher, she ascended until she was well above the trees.

Still hearing her name, she began to move toward the voice. As if drifting in warm water, she descended onto Katrina's large wraparound porch. Walking past the white wicker furniture, she was amazed at how clear and beautiful everything looked. Instead of opening the door, she walked through it and into the sitting room.

Peter and Katrina appeared to be in some kind of trance. Their eyes were closed, and they were not speaking, but she could hear every word they were thinking. Sitting in a chair, she whispered, "I've come."

Katrina opened her eyes. "She's here," she spoke slowly and quietly, "Do you sense it?"

"Yes," he said slowly, "I believe I feel her also."

Katrina spoke some unfamiliar words. They seemed to be in a foreign language, and yet she understood them and found herself answering. "Yes, I will do as you say."

"Very good," Katrina whispered.

"Can you see her?" Peter asked in a soft voice.

Joan watched as Katrina stood and moved towards her. She walked behind the chair that Joan was sitting in and placed her hands on both sides of Joan's head.

"Not with my eyes," she answered, "but yes, my soul sees her perfectly."

"Joan," Katrina spoke in a kind beguiling voice, "I want you to go to Peter. I want you to embrace him."

In obedience, Joan left her chair, sat on Peter's lap, and began to caress him. She ran her fingers through his hair before covering his face with kisses.

Peter sighed.

"That's enough Joan," Katrina said.

Joan stood, and Peter opened his eyes.

"It is Joan," Katrina assured Peter. "She is still with us, but we are her teachers and we must educate her. If we fail, our leader will choose someone else. It's time for the one we have been waiting for to be born of a woman." She raised her voice and called, "Joan! I'm sending you back now. Go back to the bench, and then come to us wearing your body."

The stone bench was hot, and Joan's clothes were wet with perspiration.

She sat up trying to get her bearings. Dazed and confused, she looked around, attempting to focus on her watch. *What a strange dream...What time is it? Peter and Katrina must be wondering what happened to me.*

Walking toward the house, her legs felt shaky. *What's wrong with me? Am I getting sick? I must have been in the sun too long.*

As she approached the house, she found Katrina and Peter sitting on the porch in the white wicker chairs drinking something in ice-filled glasses.

"There she is!" Katrina called.

"I...I'm sorry. I don't know what happened to me. I guess I fell asleep."

Peter and Katrina laughed in unison.

"Come sit down," Peter said. "Would you like some iced tea? You've had quite an afternoon!"

Joan frowned in confusion. "Yes, yes, thank you. I had the strangest dream."

The two laughed at the shared joke, and Joan looked bewildered.

"It wasn't a dream," Katrina said, looking into Joan's eyes. "It really happened."

"It happened...what...how?" She looked from one face to the other.

Katrina took her hand. "Remember how I've been telling you there is a deeper truth...that there is one who is in control of the earth? He is the one we serve."

Joan was confused but nodded as she concentrated on trying to understand.

"He's taught us we can leave our bodies and do his bidding."

She stared at them, still not sure she understood. "This is hard to believe," she finally answered.

"I gave you something in the juice to help you relax and go to sleep but also to bring you into another realm of consciousness. You left your body, and you came to us when I called to you. Is this true?"

"Yes," she whispered, bewildered.

"You were able to fly above the trees, to walk through walls, and read minds...is that also correct?"

"Yes."

"Did you experience this," Joan asked Peter. "Did you understand what was happening?"

"With my eyes closed I would have sworn you were sitting on my lap!" he laughed.

Joan dropped her head and studied her hands. "What does this mean?" She looked up at Peter, "You're *not* new to this as you pretended, are you?"

"I'm sorry I didn't tell you before," he said, "But we had to make sure you were the one."

She looked at them and was bewildered. "The one?"

Katrina turned to Joan. "The world needs a leader, Joan, someone who will take control and cause things to progress in the right direction. Our leader has a plan. A woman must give birth to a child who will be trained from infancy. By the time your child is a man, the world will be ready to receive him. Are you willing to have a child that will one day rule the world?"

"I…I guess anyone would answer yes, but how is this possible?"

Katrina stood and began walking back and forth speaking in a loud voice as if she were giving a lecture. "From the beginning of time, time as we know it, and actually before time, we have been in a war. He…our enemy, sent his son to try and win the battle against us. But," at this she whirled around dramatically, her eyes sparking, "we will also have a son. He will be a man who is kind and tolerant, and very handsome and he'll have all of the answers because he will have the wisdom of the ages!"

Joan listened intently, not sure she understood.

He'll be well-educated, and his words will mesmerize. He will be wealthy and have great powers of persuasion. At first, he will seem to be just like everyone else, but then he will quickly move up the political ladder."

A fire she could not comprehend was burning in Joan's chest as Katrina continued.

"Everyone will look to him for answers. And because he will appear to give them, they will do whatever he asks. People are already disillusioned, but by the time he is a man, they will be ready for a change, no matter what the price."

Peter was listening in rapt attention practically on the edge of his seat, agreeing with every word.

"The economy will be in ruins, but he will have the answers. There will be hardships greater than mankind has ever known, disease and plagues, but once again, he will have the answers. He'll be worshiped and honored and, as his mother, you will also be honored. Think of it Joan, you will be the mother of the most powerful man in the world, the most powerful man that has ever lived. He will be our messiah, and no one will be able to stop us."

Joan looked at Peter. She was shaking as he took her hand, "Our son?" she asked bewildered.

Katrina interrupted, "It will appear he is Peter's son, and yes, you will give birth to him, but he will not be Peter's son."

Joan looked at Katrina not understanding, fearing if she understood, she would not be able to agree.

"He'll be our ruler incarnate and he'll rule, as no one has ever ruled before."

Katrina's voice was getting louder and louder until Joan wanted to cover her ears and scream for her to be silent. Instead, she sat motionless, held captive by Katrina's voice that reverberated inside of her head as if Katrina was speaking through a loudspeaker. But then Joan felt as if she could not bear another word. Katrina lowered her voice to almost a whisper, looked deep into Joan's eyes and said, "Joan, will you say yes to the ruler of the universe? Will you agree to give birth to Lucifer's son?"

Not able to move, Joan stared at her as if she was in a hypnotic trance.

"If you refuse, we will find another! I'll wipe your mind clean of every memory of this day, but we can wait no longer, it's time for this child to be born! We must have your full consent and cooperation, or the honor will go to another. Are you willing to have Lucifer's child?"

Joan heard the words coming out of her mouth involuntarily. She covered her mouth as if somehow, she could stop them. "Yes!" she said. "Yes, I will have this child. But how will this happen."

The diabolical look in Katrina's eyes sent chills down her spine. She looked at Peter for reassurance. He smiled and squeezed her hand again. She exhaled slowly. It seemed she had been holding her breath for a long, long time.

"In days of old, the angels that followed Lucifer mated with human women and produced the heroes of old. But this time, Lucifer himself will have a son and no one will be able to defeat him."

Joan felt as if she were about to faint, but she looked at Peter and he gave her a reassuring smile. "It's alright my love," he whispered. "Everything is going to be fine."

Chapter Seventeen

Ellen sat on the floor of the bridal shop, her mouth full of pins, measuring the hem of the store's most expensive creation.

Turning and twisting in front of the mirror, Joan admired the effect of the tight-fitting bodice with the plunging neckline and the full skirt.

"Do you really think this style makes my waist look smaller? I can't decide if I like this dress best or the one with the sweetheart neckline."

"You look beautiful in every dress you've tried on, but yes, I believe you've chosen the most becoming. Now, if you'll just stand still, I think a few more pins and I can start the alterations."

"Make sure you take it in at the waist. I know the wedding is only two weeks away, but I think I can lose another six or seven pounds."

Ellen sighed, exasperated, and tried not to compare her own five foot eleven, stocky frame to Joan's diminutive figure. Practically lying on the floor, she checked to make sure Joan's dress barely skimmed her shoes when she walked.

Sitting up, Ellen tried to pull the train out to its full length as Joan preened before the mirror.

"Ellen, telephone!" Abby called from the office.

Jumping up, Ellen prayed Joan wouldn't notice how happy she was for an excuse to leave her incessant primping.

Forgive my impatience, Lord! I know you love Joan too. Please, God, I need help with my attitude.

Tony's voice on the line brought a ready smile.

"I was hoping it was you," she bubbled. "I have some exciting news. Mary Catherine said she would go to Bible study with us tonight if she could find someone to keep Jill. Guess what? Lois volunteered! Isn't that great?" Ellen was surprised at Tony's hesitation. "Is anything wrong?"

"No...no, I'm sure she will take good care of her, It's just that…"

"It's just what?"

"I…I, oh never mind, that's wonderful news. I'll pick you up at six-thirty."

"Great, Lois can ride over with us when we go to pick up Mary Catherine." Ellen hung up the phone unsettled but not sure why. She went back to the showroom and was relieved to find Joan in the dressing room changing into her street clothes. The fitting had taken much longer than she'd anticipated, and she still had two bridesmaid dresses to hem before she could leave for the day.

As she sewed, she prayed silently. *Father, I want so much for Mary and Tony to hear things that will help them understand how much you love them. Please open their ears to hear the truth. Protect this night and everyone who will be coming to the Bible study...give Philip and Phoebe just the right words and open all of our hearts so we can receive your truth and grow.*

Concentrating on praying and sewing, she was startled when Abby tapped her on the shoulder. They both laughed when Ellen jumped at her touch.

"I didn't mean to scare you. Can you use some help?"

"That would be wonderful. I've got these two dresses pinned, but they still need to be cut off and hemmed. Tony's picking me up in an hour, and I don't see how I'll be finished."

"I'll start with the peach one. Ellen?"

"Hmmm?"

"I overheard you talking to Tony about going to a Bible study with Mary."

"Yes?"

"Well, what's it like? Do you just sit around reading the Bible? It sounds pretty boring. I've never read the Bible, but I did see the Ten Commandments. I loved that movie."

"It's a little hard to explain, but it's never boring, especially with Phoebe and Philip. For the last few weeks, we've been studying the war between good and evil. You know, between the Devil and God?"

"Do you *really* believe in the Devil? I always thought he was kind of like, well, you know, witches and goblins, ghosts and things kids dress up like…you know for Halloween. Do you think he's…real?"

"Yes, he certainly is real, but he doesn't wear a red suit and horns. He's been pretty clever over the centuries to convince people he's just a caricature or a cartoon figure."

"Where did he come from? Lois and Joan think we all came from UFOs or something like that. Joan told me the other night that there is no real devil. She said it's just a myth that Christians made up so they could control people. According to Joan, there is an alien being called Lucifer, but he's here to help us."

Ellen shook her head slowly, tried not to roll her eyes, but didn't comment.

"She said all this God stuff is just superstition and that Lucifer is the one who rules the universe. Joan says I should go with her for a reading. Joan believes Katrina is responsible for giving her favor with Peter and she wouldn't be about to marry a multi-millionaire if it wasn't for Katrina."

Ellen swallowed and frowned but still didn't comment.

"I don't know what to believe."

Not knowing what to say, Ellen prayed a quick silent prayer. *Please, God, I don't want to turn her off. Please give me the right words.*

Abby looked at Ellen, puzzled.

"Well…," Ellen said, trying to think of how she could best explain without turning Abby off, "at the Bible study I go to, we believe the Bible was written to teach people how to live and that God inspired men who loved Him to write it. That's why we call it God's Word. It's also a history of the world, and it even tells us a few things that happened before the world was ever created."

"How can anyone know what happened before the world was created?"

"The Bible says before time began, there was a war in heaven. Lucifer led one-third of the angels against God. The angels that followed Satan, or Lucifer, are what we now commonly call demons or evil spirits. I'm sorry, I've probably said a lot more than you wanted to hear." She laughed nervously, "I've got a habit of doing that on this subject."

"No, really, I think this is interesting. Maybe I'll go with you sometime. This makes a lot more sense than that garbage Joan is always spouting."

Ellen's excitement at Abby's interest quickly turned to alarm as she raised her head to find Joan standing in the doorway, eyes blazing.

"I left my sunglasses in the dressing room."

"I'll get them," Ellen said jumping up.

Abby tried to be nonchalant, "I like the dress you picked. It's so sophisticated."

Joan snatched the glasses out of Ellen's hand and stomped out of the room.

Abby blanched white, "Do you think she heard me say she spouts garbage?"

"Who knows, with Joan it could be anything. You're welcome to come with us tonight. Tony has been coming the last few weeks, and he loves it."

Abby was too shaken to concentrate. "Not tonight," she said. "Maybe some other time."

Chapter Eighteen

Joan had only meant to sleep for twenty minutes. Rolling over, she kicked the blankets to the floor, groaned, and squinted at the clock in disbelief. It was already five-twenty, and Peter would be here in less than an hour. She sat on the side of the bed, trying to get her bearings, and considered her options. Her long blonde hair, snarled from a fitful nap of tossing and turning, hung in tangled clumps, giving her the look of a sullen child.

I shouldn't have had that second glass of wine with lunch, she chastened herself. *It's almost as if I've been drugged. And the nightmares, who ever heard of having such horrid nightmares in the middle of the day?*

The residue of the dream was still fresh in her mind as she peered out of the window at the lilac bush, heavy with blossoms. The aroma was so strong, it permeated the glass and faded the horror of the haunting darkness. Outside, a redwing blackbird was singing, bringing back memories of her childhood.

Remembering the shame and the school children's rejection, she clenched her teeth. *Poverty is the real hell.* She covered her ears, hearing in remembrance the shrieking voice of her stepmother's accusations, "You're a whore and you're going to hell!"

According to my father, everyone is destined for hell, so why even try? So what if the boys paid me for my favors? I had something they wanted, and they had something I wanted...money. Telling my parents I was babysitting stopped the accusations for a while. Oh well, that was a long time ago. She studied her image in the mirror. *Stop it!* she chastised herself. *You still have what it takes to make every male give you a second look.* "Stop thinking about the past," she whispered and smiled at her reflection. *I've no reason to be concerned. If things don't work out with Peter, I can always go back to John Elwood. If my father and that hypocritical pack of Christians are right, it doesn't matter what I do. I'm on my way to hell anyway, so what difference does it make?*

A sudden flashback of her mother's sweet face momentarily disarmed her. *You loved me, Mom. Why did you have to die? I was such a little girl, and I needed you.*

I've got to stop thinking about the past. I've got to pull myself together. If only I could understand what's happening. Okay, I know Katrina drugged me, that was obvious, and maybe Peter drugged me too. But why would they drug me? No, no, I'm just being paranoid. I can't believe I really flew. It was a dream, that's all. But how did Katrina know what was in my dream? Maybe they gave me a drug, and then while I was drugged, she planted the thought of me flying in my mind, knowing I would dream what she had already suggested. I'm sure the whole flying thing was a hallucination. Katrina must have hypnotized Peter, and maybe she's been hypnotizing me too.

She sighed heavily, whispering her resolve, "I don't care what they're up to as long as it benefits me?"

Yanking at the covers, she smoothed the bedspread until every wrinkle was gone. *Someday I'll have a maid to do this.* She said in determination.

Continuing to mull over the previous day, she rummaged through boxes of shoes looking for the pair that would perfectly match her outfit.

As she dressed, she considered, *Who in their right mind would think you could have sex with a demon, or an alien, or Lucifer himself for that matter. Still, these people do have some kind of power...maybe it's all manipulation...some kind of mind control. Probably a combination of hypnosis and drugs. And another strange thing, me meeting Peter..., Peter falling in love with me, all appear to have been arranged by Katrina. But why? Why did she choose me?*

At times, Joan wanted to run, but the rewards she gained from Katrina were irresistible and reeled her back like a fish on a line.

Bathing quickly, she started on her makeup. *Okay,* she sighed, *if I have to make them believe I'll have Satan's child, so be it. The most important thing is for me to get Peter and everything I've ever wanted.*

Maybe Katrina is right, maybe the beings called demons and angels are just creatures from another sphere. She says they are in a war to control the world. It certainly seems true. Either way, I'll still have Peter. Tonight I'll meet the others, but I've nothing to fear. After all, I can always have Peter's baby and convince them it's Lucifer's child.

Joan laughed aloud and was surprised at how diabolical her voice sounded. *That was creepy! Okay, Joan, pull yourself together. At least I'm honest with myself, unlike that crazy Ellen who believes she is helping Jesus save the world. Goody-two-shoes will see she's on the wrong side when I'm sitting in the lap of luxury, and she is as poor as a church mouse. Then she'll know! Ha! I'm*

109

beginning to believe this trash myself! One thing is sure, Peter is a multi-millionaire, and I have the power to make him do whatever I want.

She laughed again and once again was startled by the unfamiliar sound in her voice. Pushing the doubts away, Joan dressed carefully, making sure everything looked perfect. A generous spray of cologne, and she was ready for Peter. She glanced in the mirror and smiled in approval at her reflection.

Chapter Nineteen

The garage was filled with people of all ages. Ellen whispered an explanation to Mary, "We used to meet in Phoebe's living room, but the Bible study grew so large we had to start meeting in their garage."

Tony glanced over at Mary Catherine. She seemed to be in awe of everything, and he wondered if this was as strange to her as it was his first time.

A middle-aged man with sandy-colored hair was softly strumming on a guitar. Tony smiled into Ellen's anxious eyes, trying to help her relax. "Everything is okay," he whispered.

A gray-haired man stepped to the front, welcomed the visitors, and then introduced his wife. "I'm not a pastor," Philip Brown explained. "Most of you know when we opened the store six years ago, some people requested a Bible study where they could ask questions. This Bible study was born out of that request."

Many were nodding and smiling.

"A quick explanation for you newcomers. We're not trying to be a church or take the place of a church. If at any time we say or do anything you are uncomfortable with, check the scriptures and ask your pastor. We try to only say what the Bible says without putting our spin on it." He hesitated a moment and then added, "But we are human, and we are learning along with you. We trust the Holy Spirit to be our teacher, so let's begin in prayer and invite Him to teach through us."

Philip motioned for a young man sitting in the front row to pray. His words were simple, but Mary Catherine felt something stirring inside of her as he prayed.

"Thank you, Lord, for bringing us together. We want to know you. We want to serve you. Open the eyes of our understanding so we will know how to love you and each other in the way you want us to. We welcome you, Holy Spirit. Please come and be our teacher. Give us revelation as we study God's word and protect us from the evil plans of the enemy. We pray all these things in the name of our Lord Jesus. Amen."

Mary was surprised to hear several people agreeing aloud with Philip as he prayed. It was a little strange to her to hear their 'amens' resonating around the room.

Tony peeked around Ellen and noticed tears running down Mary Catherine's face. He felt a lump in his own throat also but was not sure why. An electric current seemed to run through the crowd as Phoebe read scriptures and Philip explained them.

Philip was expounding on John 3:3. Phoebe read, "Jesus said, except a man be born again, he cannot enter the kingdom of God."

Someone in the back raised his hand. "Could you explain the phrase born-again? Before coming here, I thought it was just some jargon certain denominations used. I never thought about it being in the Bible."

"Well, let's look at what Nicodemus asked Jesus. 'Can a man go back into his mother's womb?' To understand, we first have to realize we're all made in three parts. Our body is one part of us. Our soul, or our thoughts and our emotions, are the second part of us, but our spirit is who we really are."

Tony was paying close attention. He could feel Ellen watching him. Wanting to reassure her, he looked at her and smiled. She let out a sigh.

Philip continued, "We wear our bodies while we are here on earth. We process information and feel emotions through our mind or our soul, but the real person we are is our spirit man. It is the spirit man that Jesus is talking about when he says you must be born again to enter the Kingdom of God. It is our spirit man who is reborn, and it is our spirit man who will live forever. When our spirit is born again, we become a brand-new creation. Anything you have ever done is now forgiven. Anything you will ever do is covered under this wonderful forgiveness package. We don't have to wait until we die and go to heaven to be in God's kingdom. We become part of his kingdom the moment we receive Jesus as our Lord and Savior.

A woman near the front raised her hand timidly.

"Yes, Helen?"

"I was just wondering. I was baptized as a young child. Truthfully, I thought that was all I had to do to make heaven, but, well, it was really because all my friends were getting baptized and, of course, I didn't want to go to hell either."

Everyone laughed, nodding their heads in understanding.

"Since I have been coming here," she paused, "I guess I'm just not sure I've been born again."

Tony's mind was racing. *Boy, can I relate. I was baptized and I try to do everything right, but I think most of the time I'm more concerned with pleasing the people around me than pleasing God. The people at this Bible study are different than anyone I've ever met. Do they really think about pleasing God all the time? God...is it possible to have that kind of relationship with you? Are you listening to me? If you are, why do I feel so alone when I pray? I want to know you the way Ellen*

114

does, the way Philip and Phoebe do! Is that even possible?

Philip stopped speaking and turned to Phoebe. "Would you like to answer her Phoebe?"

As she took the microphone, Tony felt love and acceptance, like a warm blanket folding around him. He looked sideways at Mary Catherine. She was sniffling quietly. Ellen slipped her arm around Mary's waist. "Are you okay?" she whispered.

"No, but I want to be," she smiled through her tears. "If Jesus can make me a new person, then that's what I want."

Phoebe's words were filled with tender compassion, "That's a good question, Helen. Being born of the spirit isn't necessarily an emotional experience, although our emotions are often involved; but when you are sincere, it is a very real life-changing experience. You see, when you invite Jesus to live inside of you…He does. That means you are never alone again. He can hear every prayer because He isn't far away. He now lives inside of you. It doesn't mean that everything in your life will be good from now on. It just means you will never have to face your problems alone. He will be there for you during the hard times and rejoicing with you during times of celebration. You will always have someone to give you strength and courage and to help you be who you were created to be."

A man in the back raised his hand. "Can you tell me why some people who claim to be born-again Christians are meaner and have more messed up lives than people who have never had any religious experience?"

"Yes, sadly I know what you mean." Phoebe cleared her throat, looked thoughtful, and then continued. "Just because someone invites Jesus to live inside of him doesn't mean that their old habits and old nature will instantly disappear. It's up to us to find out God's will. Our actions will be determined by our mind or our belief systems. One of the first things a new believer needs to do is to try to find out what God wants by reading God's Word and finding out how Jesus interacted with the Father."

Heads were nodding in agreement.

"If we never read God's Word or try to conform to *His* way of seeing, we won't change. You see, we have had years of living one way and now, all of a sudden, it is as if we have been plunged into a country that is foreign to us. All of the ways of the new kingdom seem strange. Even though we live in this new kingdom, we won't necessarily always have the protection of the King unless we abide by the new kingdom's way of thinking which will produce a new way of living."

A light seemed to go on as Helen began to understand. "I see, I can't expect the police to protect me if I rob a bank or keep me from having an accident if I am going thirty miles over the speed limit even if I am a citizen of a free country. To receive the protection, I have to abide by my country's way of doing things," Helen said.

"Exactly, and people don't automatically do the right thing just because they read the Bible either. Let's turn in our Bibles to Ephesians 2:8. Ellen, let's have you read."

She stood and read, "For by grace are ye saved through faith; and not by yourselves: it is the gift of God."

Ellen sat down and Phoebe continued to explain. "We don't have to be good enough to receive salvation but if we have had a true experience of receiving Jesus as our savior, we will most likely want to do what pleases Him, but God will not force us to change." Phoebe smiled at Philip as she handed back the microphone.

Philip had several others read scriptures and then said, "I think God has answered a lot of our questions tonight, and I believe the Holy Spirit is drawing us all closer to God. Let's pray and ask Jesus to come into our inner man and make us new creations. I'm sure most of you have already prayed this prayer before, but let's all pray it aloud together and reaffirm our faith. I will pray, and I would like you all to repeat this prayer with me so no one will feel embarrassed if you've never prayed this before."

In unison, the little group repeated, "Father, in the power of your Son, Jesus, and by His atoning blood, I invite you to come and live inside of me. Take away all of my sins and make me a brand-new creation. Forgive me and give me the ability to forgive everyone who has sinned against me. Teach me through your Word and give me an understanding of your ways."

Tony choked on the words as he thought of the hatred he held against the drunk driver who had killed his wife. But he said the words and he meant every one of them. As he prayed, he felt the heaviness he had carried for the last year release from his chest. He finished the prayer with the others repeating the words, "I receive you Holy Spirit and thank you for making all things in me brand new."

Tony heard little of the rest of what was going on. He had a vague sense of people singing. He felt as if he were being filled with warm honey as he continued to silently pour out his grief and pain to the Savior.

When he opened his eyes, the first one he saw was Mary Catherine with glistening tears of joy and a huge smile.

The man with the guitar started singing a lively tune. Everyone seemed to know the words and joined in. People all around him were clasping his hand and hugging him and saying how happy they were that he was coming to Bible study. He was amazed that it didn't feel odd at all to be hugged or to hug these strangers. They all felt like family. He turned and looked deep into Ellen's eyes. Taking her hand he whispered, "Thank you for bringing me here. I…I…love *this*," he added softly.

And I love you, she thought as she whispered back, "I'm glad."

Just as she was sure he was reaching out to hug her, Mary turned around bumping him aside.

"Oh, Ellen, I'm not sure I understand everything that these people are talking about, but…I prayed the prayer and…and…something has happened to me. I have never felt this…this feeling of freedom before. When we were praying about forgiving others, I suddenly realized God wanted me to forgive my father. I've not ever even considered the possibility of forgiving him! It never entered my mind. When I spoke the words of forgiveness…well…I'm not sure what happened, but it felt as if something heavy lifted off my chest."

Ellen stood grinning at the two of them. Tony was still holding her hand and she was very much aware of it. Speechless, she silently prayed, *Thank you, Lord.*

Chapter Twenty

The two-story Victorian mansion made a charming bridal shop by day, but by night, it was a little frightening. Abby made a mental note. *Let's see, I've locked all of the doors and turned off most of the lights.* She checked her watch, *Oh dear, it's getting late!*

Everyone had left the shop hours earlier. She had only intended to stay for a while, but somehow the hours slipped away.

Earlier in the day, Ellen was all in a tizzy because she didn't have time to dress the mannequin and still make her date with Tony. Abby promised Ellen she would finish the window display before leaving. Now she sat at the bottom of the stairs, holding a broken mannequin arm. "Oh dear, I don't have time for this," she moaned.

Now what? She sighed in frustration and then remembered seeing a second mannequin in the storage room on the second floor.

"Shoot!" she said bewailing the fact that this was taking much more time than she had intended.

Stomping up the stairway, she worried what Mrs. Musgrave would think if she just forgot about dressing the mannequin and went home. *But she's such a stickler for featuring the latest formal wear. Ellen and I will both be in trouble if I don't set up the window display.* The grandfather clock at the foot of the stairs chimed nine o'clock as Abby turned the handle to the storage room. She jumped as the chime sounded. *Scaredy-cat. It's just a clock.*

Abby was about to pull the chain on the single light bulb that dangled from the center of the room when she heard voices. Looking around the storage room curiously, she wondered who it could be. It sounded as if Mrs. Musgrave and whoever else was speaking were in the room with her. In the dim light that filtered in from the partially open door, Abby could barely see anything but boxes sitting everywhere.

She decided against turning on the light and tiptoed silently to the side of the room where the voices seemed louder. Carefully moving a box of hangers, she found a small square door. It was located about halfway up the wall and hinged at the top.

Why, it's a dumb waiter, she thought. *It must go to the kitchen on the first floor.* Her heart began to pound as she tried to quietly lift the hinged door so she could hear better. As she lifted the door, the hinges complained with a low-pitched squeak.

"Oh no," she whispered in fear. *If Mrs. Musgrave finds me here, she'll be so mad. She hates paying overtime, and she'll never believe I didn't intend to stay this late or to write it down on my time sheet. I'll just wait until she leaves. Surely she won't stay long.*

Although Abby's fingers were cramping from holding the door of the dumb waiter open, she was afraid the softest squeak would alert the people downstairs.

Shifting her position, she waited impatiently for Mrs. Musgrave to leave, but her foot slipped and bumped against a box of hangers. Over the hangers went with a muffled crash.

"What was that?" the voice from the wall asked.

"Don't worry, Katrina," Mrs. Musgrave answered, "the girls left hours ago. This is an old house. It's always making strange noises."

Abby groaned inwardly as she listened, barely able to breathe. Now she heard a male voice, but he was speaking so quietly she could scarcely understand a word he said.

"We can't stop now," the raspy voice said angrily. "Larry, you have to convince the captain that you have investigated our group and have found us to be perfectly above board."

"You must realize that not only you but everyone in your group is under suspicion." The

122

male voice responded. He seemed to be mumbling after that, and Abby was unable to understand what he was saying.

"But I've already told you, we had nothing to do with that!" Mrs. Musgrave retorted loudly. "Our organization was formed to help the community. Just because we don't believe the same way as those troublemakers...well...well...that doesn't make us murderers," she blustered.

"It's about time you told me everything," answered the one they called Larry.

Abby strained to hear but could only catch a few words.

"If you two are involved in these abductions, I need to know about it now. I've looked the other way...," again he lowered his voice and Abby could only catch a few words.

"We are a respected part of this community. I can't imagine why anyone would begin to accuse us," Mrs. Musgrave complained.

"And what about the child found in the park? The coroner said she appeared to have a leviathan cross carved on her chest and most of her blood had been removed."

The raspy voice was hollering now. "I said we are not murderers and this has nothing to do with us! I've warned you, Larry. If you falsely accuse me, you'll pay a price!"

Abby's fingers burned with pain, but she fearfully held the dumb waiter door open. Perspiration ran down her back as she realized what they were saying. Her heart was now pounding so loudly that she feared they could hear her in the kitchen. Although she strained to hear, the threesome was whispering, and she could only catch a few words. Sitting with one leg folded beneath her caused a loss of circulation in her left foot, but she was terrified at the bits and pieces of conversation she had heard and was afraid to move.

Out of desperation, Abby began to silently pray. *Dear God, if you are as real as Ellen says you are, please, please I need your help. I've got to get out of here.* She caught her breath at the sound of... *footsteps.*

Not daring to breathe, she held her breath. She was sure of it now. Someone was slowly walking up the stairs. As the door to the storage room slowly opened all the way, Abby crouched behind one of the boxes but then, there in the doorway, stood a policeman with a flashlight in his hand.

"Oh! Thank God, thank God," Abby cried jumping up. She pulled the chain dangling in the center of the room, turning on the overhead light. "I'm not a burglar," she started to explain, "I work here, and something terrible is going on. I'm not sure of everyone involved, but I heard a man and two women speaking and I think…"

Abby fell silent as two women came into view and one of them was Mrs. Musgrave. The policeman began to walk slowly toward her.

"What are you going to do to me?" Abby whispered as she moved backward toward the wall. In moments, it was over. Losing her balance, she went down, and as she did, her head struck a pipe that ran across the back wall. The room began to spin and fold in on her, and then everything went black.

The three stood staring as she lay motionless on the broken tile floor. Only the policeman spoke.

"Alright Katrina, I did as you asked, but now she can identify all three of us. What next?"

"You get rid of her, that's what!" Katrina answered. "And you better make sure there's no evidence."

"Is she dead," Marilyn Musgrave whispered.

Larry knelt beside her. "I can't feel a pulse."

"I said get rid of her," Katrina shrieked. "And I hope you realize that now you're in this thing as deeply as we are."

Chapter Twenty-One

Evelyn Wind was buttering toast for her husband's breakfast when the phone rang. She tightened her shoulders as she walked toward the phone on the kitchen wall. *Will they ever leave him alone?* Day and night the phone rang. Forty years ago, when she proudly embraced the position of pastor's wife, she never imagined the constant demand on her personal life or the endless interruptions of her privacy.

"Hello?"

"Oh, Evelyn, thank God you're home. Is the pastor in?"

In the shower, Evelyn thought to herself. *Can't you people ever solve your own problems?* She forced herself to be pleasant despite Judy Sand's lack of a proper hello.

"He's not available right now, Judy. Can I be of help?"

"Well…it's that girl across the street. Tony has been going with her for over a month and last night I found out he took her to some kind of meeting in a *garage,* and this morning he is acting, well, weird!"

Don Wind came out of the bathroom, pointed to himself, and questioned, "Is it for me?"

Evelyn motioned to the breakfast waiting on the table and silently mouthed the word, "eat."

Don, in obedience, sat down and began to salt his eggs as Evelyn pursed her lips and shook her head frowning in disapproval. Forty years of marriage and Evelyn was still trying to call the shots, but Don had his own little way of letting her know she wasn't in control. Eating salt against her protest was just one of them.

Evelyn sat on a stool at the kitchen counter as Judy Sands continued to ramble. If Don wasn't sitting ten feet away, she would have taken a deck of cards out of the cupboard and played solitaire.

Playing cards while someone poured out their troubles had saved her sanity on more than one occasion. She had decided long ago that people didn't want advice. They just wanted a sounding board. If you just said, "Yes" or "I understand" when you heard a pause in the conversation, they were content.

She had saved her husband hours of listening to boring, self-centered women who simply wanted a shoulder to cry on. Evelyn knew if Don had answered the phone, he would have taken an hour and a half trying to give her good scriptural advice she would never take.

Evelyn pointed toward the bedroom and mouthed, "Get dressed," as Pastor Don finished his breakfast. They were supposed to leave for their daughter Cindy's house in ten minutes. It was Timmy's birthday and Evelyn knew if she didn't guard the time they would be late again or worse yet, Don would tell her to go on ahead without him.

The voice on the other end of the line droned on. "I'm not sure, but I believe these people think that the Bible is literal and that God still wants to perform the same kind of miracles he performed thousands of years ago. They talk about faith all the time, and it's downright scary. Tony comes home saying the strangest things to me. He said they pray for the sick by laying hands on people and anointing them with oil just like they did in the New Testament. Can you believe it? He thinks sometimes people actually believe they are healed!"

Evelyn's ears perked up in attention. She desperately needed to be healed. The pain in her back made every day an endurance trial. *If only I could be without pain so I could enjoy my grandchildren. If only I could pick up little Timmy or work in my garden again. Oh Father, is that possible? The doctors say, apart from medication to block the pain, they have no answers. Father, do you care that I'm in pain?* Aloud she said, "Did he say he saw someone healed?"

"He said he did! How can I prove it's all fake when he is so sure he saw healings with his own eyes? I think they're probably actors to make people believe so that they'll give them money."

"Did Tony say people pay them money?"

"Well, no, he would never say that, but why else would they be holding these meetings? It must be some kind of hypnotism or something. Don't you think?"

"I don't know, but I'll talk to Don about it and get back to you. I'm sorry, but I have to go now."

Evelyn hung up the phone, surprised at the flutter of hope she felt inside. *Oh God, if only healing was for today. I don't want a lot. I'm seventy years old. I just want to leave this ministry. I am so tired of it all. I just want to have my husband's company. I just want to enjoy growing some flowers and having conversations with people who want to talk about something besides themselves and all of their trials and how hard their life is.*

Evelyn stood slowly, the pain in her back making her grimace. *Oh God, if there is some way...some way.* Contemplating all Judy had said, Evelyn walked to the bedroom to hurry Don along.

Chapter Twenty-Two

During the night, Abby had a vague recollection of an elderly woman sitting with her, putting an ice pack on her head, making her take an aspirin with a glass of water, and telling her she had merely been knocked unconscious but would be fine by morning. Now it all seemed like a strange dream or perhaps a nightmare.

Raising herself to a sitting position, she began to take inventory of her surroundings. First of all, her head hurt something awful. She rubbed the bump on the back of her head and groaned, remembering she must have passed out cold when she fell. Taking inventory, she was thankful her head wasn't bleeding. That was good. She pushed herself up on one elbow. Someone had placed her on an old cot. It smelled moldy, and when she touched the scratchy wool blanket that covered the cot, a thin puff of dust made her sneeze. She shuddered as her memory vividly flashed back to the last scene before she lost consciousness.

Looking around the room, she saw the walls were made of cement blocks. The ceiling and even the floor appeared to be made of concrete. She surmised the room to be about twelve-foot square. It had no windows. A small kerosene lamp was burning on a low table beside the cot. On the table was a pitcher of water, a bottle of aspirin and a glass. As her eyes grew accustomed to the dim light, she realized there was a door in the room made of iron or some type of metal. In the corner of the room was an antique rocker. Across from the rocker was a...a...? She was puzzled at first. *Is that a chamber pot?* She had only seen them in pictures. The ceiling seemed to be about eight or more feet above the floor, and in the center of the ceiling, there was a single grate.

I'm alive! I'm in some kind of prison, but I'm alive. She looked up at the grate in the ceiling. *That must be for ventilation,* she reasoned, *but it most certainly leads...somewhere.* She walked to the door on shaking legs. The cold cement floor assaulted her bare feet. *Where are my shoes?* she wondered.

She turned the door handle, but the result was as she expected, *locked!* Trembling from head to toe, she sat in the rocking chair, weak with terror, and looked around the room. Peeking out from under the bed, she found her shoes, and at the foot of the cot, someone had placed a man's jacket. She put the jacket and shoes on and sat back down in the rocker, puzzled.

Why did they lock me up? They probably know I heard them talking about the missing children, but I didn't hear them say they were responsible. I don't know what they were saying when they were whispering. If I can identify them and they are responsible, why would they keep me alive? Why would they make sure I had something for my head and something to keep me warm? Why did they give me a light, and why aren't I tied up? They must be pretty sure I can't escape. She stood peering at the grate in the ceiling. *There must be a way...*

Setting the contents of the table on the floor, Abby placed the table on the cot and climbed up. Reaching toward the ceiling, she was still too far from the grate to even touch it.

"Oh God, please help me," she whispered and climbed down.

Next, she studied the rocker. She decided to try and wedge the wool blanket under the end of the rockers so the chair wouldn't tip. She pushed on the rocker and analyzed its stability. *It seems to be steady. God, please make this work, please, please,* she begged as she climbed the makeshift tower. Moving carefully, she made her way to the top. As she reached for the grate, the rocker swayed and shifted forward. The table reeled, but by this time,

Abby had her fingers in the grate. Surprisingly, it was wood, not metal, but was screwed in tightly. *Oh God, please, please, what next?* The chair moved again, and this time Abby could not steady its upheaval. The blanket shifted from Abby's weight and down they came, table, chair, and Abby crashing to the floor.

"Oh-h-h-h," she wailed in pain as she lay on the cement floor. Moving her arms and legs, she affirmed nothing was broken. She'd landed on the side of her hip and her left side screamed out in accusation of her folly. Falling hard, she'd bounced on the cot as she flew through the air, and the cot had slowed her fall and buffered her landing.

The table lay on its side seemingly intact, but the chair on its back bore the brunt of the fall. A broken rocker and splintered spindles lay on the floor. Abby sat up, put her face in her hands, and cried.

Exhausted from crying and her fall, she lay back down on the cot. Still staring at the grate as a possible escape, she decided to try another tactic. Perhaps someone could hear her. Standing on the cot, she began to scream toward the grate, "Help! Help! Help me! Help me please, somebody help me!" A noise at the door stopped her.

She jumped from the bed, backed toward the farthest wall, and held her breath. The door opened slowly, and a stocky middle-aged man entered cradling a rifle under one arm. He was followed by the small elderly woman who had cared for her in the night. She was carrying a basket of food.

The woman smiled and set the basket on the floor. "Here you go darlin', I bet you're hungry." Looking around, the woman noticed the broken rocker and sighed heavily. "Might as well stop that hollerin', darlin'. I know you're scared, but nobody can hear you down here. I'm supposed to tell you that this will all be over soon. Just be patient." She looked puzzled as she noticed the pieces of the broken chair. She picked them up and shook her head. "Now why in the world did you break your chair?"

The man holding the gun seemed simple and for a minute, Abby wondered if she could wrestle the gun from him and take the two of them. Searching their faces, she was bewildered. Neither seemed particularly evil. The woman reminded her of her grandmother. "What are you going to do to me?" she asked. "And why am I here?"

At first, neither answered. In fact, they acted as if they were baffled by her question and weren't sure what to say.

"Please, what are you going to do to me?" she said louder.

"First off, we're goin' to feed you." The woman smiled. "Now, just calm down and in a little while we'll be back to check on you. I know you're scared, but hopefully this will be over soon."

"But...who are you? Why am I here?"

"Well, I guess you could say you're in protective custody. I'm sorry darlin' but you have accidentally heard and seen some things that are a threat to your life. You've been rescued, but I can't tell you any more than that. How is your head? I was told to ask you."

Abby rubbed the back of her head and answered, "I'll be all right, but where am I?"

Once again, they both ignored the question and instead answered her previous question. "I'm Mrs. Kelly and this is my son Howard. We've been hired to take care of you."

"But I SAID WHERE AM I!" she screamed in frustration.

"Now calm down and have some lunch. We'll be back shortly." With that, they left.

Abby sat back down on the bed, but the smell of food filled the tiny cell and Abby suddenly realized she was ravenously hungry. Removing the cloth covering the food and still suspicious of their intent, she wondered if it was poisoned. There was fried chicken, rolls, salad, and a piece of apple pie. *If I'm going to escape, I've got to keep my strength up. Oh, dear God, I hope they haven't poisoned this food.* Picking up a piece of chicken she began to eat.

Chapter Twenty-Three

It was an hour past opening before Mrs. Musgrave asked where Abby was.

Puzzled, Ellen wrinkled her brow in thought, "Maybe she read the schedule wrong."

The two often shared a ride, but Abby's car was gone this morning, and Ellen thought perhaps she'd left early to run errands.

Now she tried to remember if she'd seen Abby's car in front of the house last night, but all she could remember was being deliriously happy. The details of her homecoming were blurred by the joy. The only thing she recalled for sure was Tony squeezing her hand lovingly as she started to leave his car. She hoped she'd not read too much into that simple gesture.

Forcing herself to listen to Mrs. Musgrave's monologue on responsibility, Ellen shifted her weight from one foot to the other.

Pursing her lips, Mrs. Musgrave continued her rant. "I see I may have to let her go. I expected more from her. Where is her loyalty, her work ethic? If she can't go to class and still show up for work on time, we'll just have to replace her."

Turning in disgust, she marched back to her office.

Ellen completed the window display, all the while wondering why Abby had left before it was finished. *She is always responsible,* she mused. *This judgment against her is completely unfair.*

The phone rang in the office, but Ellen paid little attention. Mrs. Musgrave usually answered it.

The clunk, clunk of high heels caused Ellen to look up. Mrs. Musgrave stood in the doorway of her office, peering over her glasses in disapproval. "Ellen, there is a gentleman on the phone for you."

Ellen nodded and rushed to take the call. Her hands wet with perspiration, she picked up the receiver.

"Ellen?"

"Yes?" The butterflies started at the sound of his voice.

"Are you free for lunch?"

"What time?"

"Is one okay?"

"Perfect."

"I'll pick you up in front of the shop?"

"That will be great."

Ellen tried to ignore Mrs. Musgrave's disapproving look and her tapping foot but was stopped by the harsh comment to her retreating back. "Remember, Ellen, we are to keep personal phone calls for emergencies only."

"Yes, ma'am," Ellen said. She turned, made eye contact, and spoke sincerely to her employer. "I'm sorry. I'll speak to him about calling here."

She started to leave the room again and then turned back. "Mrs. Musgrave, I'm concerned about Abby. It's not like her not to call if she's been held up or can't make it to work. I'm really worried that something is wrong."

Mrs. Musgrave shrugged her shoulders, sighed, and went back to ignoring Ellen's remarks.

A customer called from the fitting room for assistance, and Ellen hurried to the back of the store. She was just walking to the front when the door opened. A police officer came in, looked around nervously, and then went into Mrs. Musgrave's office. He closed the door, and Ellen heard angry muffled voices, but she couldn't discern what was being said.

The morning seemed to drag on after Tony's phone call. She wanted to start on the day's alterations, but without Abby there to watch the front desk, she wasn't sure what to do. Mrs. Musgrave was still closeted in her office with the police officer, and the store was filling up with ladies wanting her attention.

At ten till one, Ellen looked at the closed door and began to panic. *I'll have to tell her I'm leaving.*

Please, Lord, give me the courage to knock on her door. I know she lumps Abby and me in the same category...and she is certainly angry at Abby.

About to knock, she heard Mrs. Musgrave's commanding voice. "This better be the end of it, Larry." She couldn't hear the officer's reply, but she scurried away from the door quickly. The police officer almost knocked her down in his apparent hurry to leave.

Catching the look on Ellen's face, Mrs. Musgrave dismissed her with a wave of her hand. "It's nothing to be alarmed at, Ellen. I'm having some problems with my neighbors...too noisy."

"Is it alright if I go to lunch now?"

"Yes, yes, go ahead." She motioned toward Ellen as if she were shooing flies. "I said go!"

Thankful to leave, Ellen grabbed her sweater and hurried out of the building. Sliding into the front seat beside Tony, she tried not to burst into tears. His smile turned to concern when he saw her expression. "Are you okay?"

"Yes, I think so. I'm just so worried about Abby. She didn't show up for work today, and it's just not like her. Can we drive by the house and see if her car's there?"

As they rounded the corner, Ellen's heart sank. The driveway was empty.

"Where to next," Tony asked.

"Let's see, can we just drive around the campus? I'm sure she didn't have a class today, but maybe you could pass by the Library."

The little blue car was nowhere in sight, and now it was too late to go to lunch.

"I'm so sorry, Tony. I know this isn't the lunch you planned."

"Can we try for supper?" He took her hand, trying to reassure her. "Maybe she had a doctor's appointment. Maybe she just looked at the schedule wrong."

Ellen nodded, "Maybe, but I think she would have called the shop or at least told me. Do you think I should call the police?"

"Not yet, there's probably a logical explanation."

"Yes, yes, you're right, of course, and I'd love to have supper with you tonight. This will probably all be resolved by then," she said, trying to smile.

Heading back into work, she determined she would trust God, but she couldn't seem to shake the feeling of impending doom.

Dear God, help me, she prayed as she entered the bridal shop. For some reason, the old house seemed gloomy, even a little eerie. The morning sunshine had disappeared, and thick rain clouds made everything look dark and depressing. Ellen sighed and tried to concentrate on shortening the

dress in front of her, but she could only think of
Abby and wonder where she was.

Chapter Twenty-Four

Mary Catherine stretched as she woke from another restful night's sleep. The past few days she'd felt as if nothing could ever be wrong again. Pushing the button on the alarm clock to off, she rolled over.

I'm brand new, she thought, savoring the memory of Tuesday's Bible study. *The past is gone and I'm a brand new person.* She placed her hand on her growing abdomen. "You have a brand new mommy, Baby," she whispered to the tiny child growing inside of her.

Jill's pat-patting footsteps announced her arrival. Standing beside the bed in her flannel-footed pink pajamas, she smiled at her mother who was pretending to be asleep. Opening her eyes, Mary feigned surprise, laughed, and then invited Jill to join her. The little girl climbed into bed, giggling in anticipation of being cuddled and tickled as she snuggled under the covers.

"Come here, you," Mary teased affectionately as she pulled Jill close. "Did you come to wake me up?"

"Yes," Jill squealed happily.

"Guess what? Today after daycare I am going to take you to the zoo, then we'll buy groceries, and then...," she hesitated for emphasis.

"We'll make cookies?" Jill asked eagerly.

"Yes, we will, so you better hurry and pick out what you want to wear, and I'll be right in to help you dress."

~~~

The day had been as amazing as Mary anticipated, but now a tired Jill and Mary Catherine stood on their front porch. Mary, fumbling with her keys, tried to balance a sack of groceries in one hand and her purse in the other. *What a wonderful day we've had,* she thought as she turned the key in her front door. Jill stood waiting patiently as the key finally found its target. The phone sounded as they entered.

"Jill, can you get the phone for Mommy? This sack is about to break."

The little girl ran for the phone, thrilled to be treated like a grown-up.

Walking into the bedroom, Mary Catherine watched, amused. Jill was nodding her head yes to whatever question was being asked. Mary took the phone from her whispering, "Thank you, Miss Secretary. I'll take over for now…Hello?"

"Mary, it's Ellen. I don't have long to talk. Tony is taking me to dinner, but I wanted to see how you're doing."

"Oh Ellen, I can't tell you what a wonderful day I've had. Jill and I just got back from the zoo, and earlier I went to lunch with Judy and Lois. I've been so happy lately. They both noticed, so I told them about the wonderful Bible study. I'm not sure they understood what I was talking about, but I'm not sure I understand either," she laughed. "How's Tony? I can hardly wait until next week. Philip makes everything so easy to understand."

Mary continued asking questions excitedly, not realizing she wasn't waiting for answers.

"Actually, I haven't talked to Tony about Tuesday. I've been waiting for him to bring it up and truthfully Mary, I've been so worried about Abby that I can't think of anything else."

"Why, what happened?"

"She didn't come home last night, and no one has seen her today either."

Mary was silent for a moment, trying to digest the information. "Is this unusual for her? Does she have a boyfriend? Could she be with family?"

"No, she doesn't have a boyfriend. Her mother lives on the East Coast. I don't think they're very close. She never mentions family. She moved here to go to school, and she started working at the bridal shop about the same time I did. Mary, I'm really concerned. Abby's not like this; she's always very transparent about everything and very responsible."

"Should we call the police?"

"Tony thinks it's premature. Will you pray for her?"

"Well, I'm not sure I know how, but I guess I can try. I'm kind of new at this, you know."

"Mary, just talk to God the way you would to anyone. He wants to hear what you have to say."

"It's that simple?"

"Yes, it's that simple."

"Okay, I can do that."

"I'll keep you posted. I'm trying not to make a big deal out of this, but with all the strange things that have been happening with the missing children and…"

"Yes, I know." They were both silent for a moment.

"Well, here's Tony. I better go."

Hanging up the phone, Mary sat down hard on her bed. She could hear Jill singing to herself as she played in the next room.

"Dear God, I'm just beginning to get to know you, but Ellen and Phoebe say you care about everyone, and I believe that's true. Last Tuesday night, you wiped my slate clean. Before I say anymore, I want to thank you for loving me and for giving me the best days I can ever remember. I have a request. I'm kind of new at this, as you know, but will you please help Abby? Wherever she is, please, Lord, bring her home safely. God, I felt your love for the first time. Please let Abby feel that love too. I guess that's all for now, God. So…so…good-bye…I mean amen."

She reached for the Bible that was lying on her nightstand. "I have a P.S., God," she whispered. "Ellen says this is your special letter to me. If that's true, will you please show me where to read?" She reached for her glasses, opened up the Bible, and began to read.

Chapter Twenty-Five

Joan sighed as she finished the last of the typing. Opening the door to Peter's office, she held up the letters. He was on the phone but motioned her in.

Sitting in his over-stuffed leather chair, she looked around, observing the beautiful wainscoting and massive mahogany desk. *This will be my husband and finally everyone will have to look up to me.* She smiled.

Peter hung up the phone and moved around the desk. Taking her by the hand, he pulled her up into his arms. "I've good news," he whispered while holding her close. "The house we looked at yesterday, the one you fell in love with, will be ours by the end of the month!"

"Oh, Peter, that's wonderful!" She kissed him passionately, visualizing the fountain in the front yard, the winding staircase, and the two stories of glass that overlooked Lake Michigan.

"Another thing, I've set up a checking account and a credit card for you. I never want you to be concerned about what you buy or 'how you'll pay for it. I want you to have the freedom to express yourself as you furnish our new home or anything else that you fancy."

"It's hard to believe I'll be your wife in just a week!"

"Have you heard from your sister?"

"Yes, she's very grateful for the plane ticket. Thank you for flying her in for the wedding."

"Are you sure you don't have any other relatives you want to invite?"

"I am very sure," she answered and made a face, but her head was on his chest and Peter didn't see the disgust in her expression. *Yes, my darling, that is one thing I know. You can never meet my family. I would be mortified if you saw the shack I was raised in or met my father with his seedy, outdated clothes…or my stepmother with her perpetual odor of stale food and perspiration.* Joan groaned involuntarily at the thought of it.

"What's wrong, Sweetheart?"

"I'm sorry, nothing"s wrong, everything's perfect. I guess I was just thinking of all the things I have to do to get ready for the wedding," she lied.

"Well, since this is your last day as a working woman, maybe you'll have more time to shop. You're not regretting giving up a career as my executive secretary to be my wife, are you?" he teased.

"I think I can handle the transition," she said, laughing at his banter.

The receptionist interrupted with a message on the intercom. "There's a Mrs. Polworth to see you in the lobby, Mr. Ellington."

"Thank you, Janet. Send her in."

"Your doctor's appointment verified that you are not pregnant?"

Joan nodded.

Peter looked at Joan intently. "And you know what comes next. Are you ready for this?"

"I think so," she answered seriously.

"Tonight, we will have the wedding. This will be the real ceremony. The other one, the one in the church, is just for the community. After tonight, everything will be different between us. I won't be allowed to touch you as my wife until we've verified that on this night you've conceived the promised child."

"But what if…"

He placed his finger on her lips, hushing what she might say. "It will be as our leader has ordained, you will…"

The door opened, and Katrina came in, a strange glow in her eyes. "Isn't this exciting?" She was almost giddy with anticipation. "Tonight, you two will embrace your destiny," she said, walking toward them.

Joan could hardly breathe. A mixture of exhilaration and fear filled her from head to toe. Taking Joan's hand, Katrina tucked it around her arm and patted her hand in reassurance. "Don't worry little one. Tonight, you will give yourself to the one we serve, and you will be one of us in completion. You have a wonderfully exciting life ahead of you, Joan!"

Joan blinked nervously but tried to give a reassuring smile.

Peter, sensing her fear, gave her a reassuring hug. "Don't be afraid, I have something in the limo to help us all relax."

"Oh Peter," Joan exclaimed delightedly at the prospect of taking the limo, "I've never ridden in a limo before."

"Oh, my dear, you will have many trips in the limo, especially on important occasions, and tonight will be one of the most important nights of your life."

She smiled into his eyes, gaining the confidence she needed to proceed. *I wonder what I'll be asked to do. Whatever it is, it can't be that hard. I'm sure I won't have a problem seducing Peter once we're married. He hasn't been able to resist me even once over the last few months.*

Entering the limo, she could feel the disapproval emanating from Katrina, and as she turned to sit, she saw the look of evil on her benefactor's face.

"Don't think for a minute that I can't read your every thought." She glared at Joan, spitting out the words. "This isn't a game, Joan. We can stop right now if you like. I'm sure the council will be happy to choose another."

Joan's skin crawled, and her limbs felt as if they were filled with ice water. "How did you…"

"Know what you were thinking? Don't be so naïve, Child. Your thoughts are no secret to me." She patted Joan's hand. "Give her some of that wine, Peter. She needs to relax."

Joan took the wine as medicine, gulping it down, and in moments, it was evident the wine had been laced. After a few swallows, a feeling of euphoria enveloped her, and everything took on a pleasant fuzzy glow.

The driver headed out of town, and the countryside flew by as Joan gazed out the window. Much too soon, they arrived at their destination. More than twenty cars were parked in the drive, on the grass, and alongside the road leading to the country home.

Joan's legs were weak as she leaned on Peter's arm. They were greeted by several well-dressed men and women holding cocktail glasses. Entering the foyer, Joan couldn't help but notice

151

that the inside of the home was lavishly decorated, while the outside seemed modest in comparison.

As they entered the house, a tall blonde woman came forward and kissed her cheek. "At last we meet," she whispered as she took Joan's arm. "Don't be afraid, I'm here to serve you. My name is Rhonda, and I'll be your personal attendant. I'll help you with your garments."

"Garments?"

"Clothing, your ceremonial robes," Rhonda explained.

Leading Joan into the bedroom, she closed the door. "It's your wedding dress, Dear. Don't be afraid."

Rhonda unzipped a garment bag and took out a lavishly embellished red velvet gown. A goat's head and other strange symbols were embroidered with threads of silver and gold on each piece of clothing.

The effects of the drug-laden wine continued to keep Joan in a euphoric dreamy state. "Maybe this is just a dream," she said, not realizing she spoke aloud until Rhonda answered her, sneering.

"Yes, life is a dream," she laughed hollowly. "This is all just a dream, and we must leave these bodies to be who we really are. You'll soon find the truth. Katrina will guide you as she has guided all of us."

Helping Joan change her clothing, Rhonda stared at her for a moment. "Yes, you will do nicely," she said, studying Joan's form with admiration. "You look lovely. The spirits will be well pleased."

After helping Joan, Rhonda donned her own red velvet robe. It was embroidered with dragons and many of the same symbols as Joan's garment, but not nearly as elaborate. "It's time," she said. "Everyone is waiting."

Chapter Twenty-Six

The telephone rang four times before Mary could get her eyes open. The voice on the other end sounded shaky and frightened.

"Mary?"

"Yes?"

"It's Ellen."

Mary held her breath, fearing the worst.

"It's been over 48 hours, and we still can't find Abby."

"Have you talked to the people at the college?"

"Yes, her professors and also some of her classmates," she said sighing deeply.

"No one has seen her?"

"No one."

"What's next?"

"Tony and I are going to the police department. Do you want to come?"

"I have Jill and…"

"Would she like a play date with Jen?"

"She would love it!"

"Tony's cleared it with his mom. He suggested the girls play at his house."

"What time are you going?"

"Is ten o'clock, okay? I don't want to take your whole Saturday."

"It doesn't matter. Ellen?"

"Yes?"

"This probably sounds strange, but I feel she's going to be found and she's going to be okay. I've been praying as you asked me, and…well…it's hard to explain, but I feel very peaceful about all of this. I hope it's not because she's…already gone."

"I keep thinking if only I'd canceled my date with Tony. I was so selfish. Something must have occurred after she left work…if only I'd stayed at work, none of this would have happened."

"You can't blame yourself. I went through this 'if only' thing with Mark. Believe me, it doesn't do any good. If we're trusting God, maybe we should stop speaking and thinking the worst."

The silence on the other end made Mary feel uncomfortable. She was afraid she'd overstepped the boundaries of her new friendship. "Are you okay?"

"Yes, I guess I was just thinking that what you are telling me, I should be a mature enough Christian to say to you. Do you think we should even go to the police?"

155

"It can't hurt, but I think we have to realize whether or not the police help us…well, I guess what I'm trying to say is, after all is said and done, we still have to trust God to help us."

The young women said their goodbyes and Mary Catherine went in to wake Jill. The memory of yesterday's headline brought her attention back to the grieving parents of the two missing children. Trying to recall the names of the children, she decided to check the paper before waking her daughter. *Maybe there will be more information…*

Details about Child Emerge.

The parents of Brenda Harrison continue to deny any knowledge of the circumstances leading to the death of their two-year-old toddler. Raymond Harrison, the father of the child, told reporters today that there was no sign of a break-in. The doors and windows were all locked, and the child seemingly just disappeared. Authorities believe the death occurred shortly after she disappeared on March 9th. The decomposition was probably delayed by the unusually cold spring weather. County Coroner, Ted Mason, reported to the authorities that the child was already dead from an overdose of barbiturates before the satanic symbol was cut on her chest. Coroner Mason revealed on Thursday that the knife marks made only a slight indentation in the skin with no blood, proving the symbol was cut post-mortem.

Mary Catherine closed the paper and sat at the kitchen table trembling. "Father," she whispered, "please, please, stop this evil. I know I'm just beginning to know you, but I know you hate this. Please, help the Harrisons. Somehow, God, give them the comfort that only you can give. Please let them know that this did not happen because of you. Please put a stop to the evil that is destroying our community." Mary covered her face with her hands and let the tears flow. *Dear God, I don't know how they can bear it. Please, Father, send someone to help them in the same way you sent someone to help me.*

Raising her head, she took a tissue from her robe pocket, blew her nose, and went to the sink to fill the teakettle. Hearing footsteps behind her, she froze, gasped, and then smiled down at the disheveled little girl standing behind her.

"Hello Sleepyhead, guess what? You've been invited to have a playdate at Jennifer's house this morning. Mommy is going to run errands with Tony and Ellen. Doesn't that sound like fun?"

"Yes!" she cried in delight and clapped her little hands.

"I'll make your breakfast first," Mary said as she took the cereal out of the cabinet. "Oh God, how can they stand it?" she whispered as she watched her own little angel dancing and twirling in excitement. *If this happened to Jill, I couldn't go on living.*

God, I don't understand what's happening. Did the same devilish mind that took the Harrison child take Abby? We need your help, Lord. We need your answers.

While Jill ate her breakfast, Mary absentmindedly reached for the Bible she'd left lying on the table last night. Opening it up at random, she silently prayed for the comfort she so badly needed.

Chapter Twenty-Seven

The police officer looked at Tony suspiciously. "And what relation did you say you are to the missing girl?"

"No relation, she's my neighbor, she lives across the street."

"And you?" he spoke to Ellen.

"No relation, she's my friend, and we rent a house with two other women."

"Hmmm," the officer replied as he wrote something in a notebook. "She is an adult," he added as he continued to write. "You say her car and purse are missing also?"

"Yes, but it's not like her to…to just take off like this."

The middle-aged officer shifted his weight and looked at them with little concern. "Don't you think you're worried over nothing?" he asked. "After all, she's twenty-two years old, hardly a child. Have you called any of her relatives or anyone who might know if she had plans to leave town?"

"I've only known her a short time, but I know she's an only child and her mother is a widow." She sighed and slowly shook her head. "I don't even have her mother's phone number."

"We could probably ask at the school," Mary Catherine suggested, "but I'm not sure they'd give us her personal information."

Ellen's eyes pooled with tears as she tried to keep her composure. "A lot of strange things are happening in this town," she said to the police officer. "I don't see how we can take this disappearance lightly."

He sighed and shuffled some papers, but it was evident he wasn't about to take her seriously.

Tony placed his arm around Ellen's shoulders and whispered, "I think we should go."

The officer stood, dismissing them, but finally addressed Ellen with a bit of compassion. "I'm sorry about your friend, Miss. I know you're worried, but at this point, there's nothing we can do. If you haven't heard from her in forty-eight hours, come back and file a formal complaint. Young women her age decide impulsively to run off with some guy or…"

"Not Abby!" Ellen shouted. She looked around embarrassed as several people in the office stopped what they were doing and stared at her. "Not Abby," she said, lowering her voice to a whisper. "And it has already been over forty-eight hours."

He glared at her for a few seconds and then dropped his gaze. Rubbing his temple, he tried to explain, "Right now we've two missing children and a murder. We just don't have the manpower to look for this woman, especially when it looks like she most likely took off of her own volition. Her car is gone, her purse is gone, and..."

"Yes, yes, I understand," Ellen said meekly, realizing her insistence was getting her nowhere. "Thank you," she added and turned to leave.

"Now what?" Tony asked the two women as they left the station.

"Well, we might find some information at the Office of Administration, but it won't be open until Monday. Could we go to the Bible bookstore? Maybe Phoebe has some ideas," Ellen offered.

Mary Catherine remained silent as they walked toward the car. *Dear God, we need your help,* she prayed silently. *We don't know where to go or what to do. Please, give us the ability to think the thoughts you want us to have, and please give Ellen your peace.*

"It's funny," Ellen said, as she waited for Tony to unlock the car. "Somehow I feel better, and even though the officer was no help, I still have faith that we're going to find her."

"I agree," Tony said.

Smiling at her two friends, Ellen added, "I'm sorry for the way I acted back there. Everything felt so hopeless, but just now as we were walking back to the car, well, nothing has changed, but I feel differently about everything."

"Well, for one thing, I've been praying for you," Tony volunteered.

"Me too," Mary added meekly.

Ellen looked at her friends in surprise. "You two are pretty amazing!"

"I wanted to tell you something," Tony said. "I woke up early this morning, and I prayed for a while and then I opened my Bible. I haven't even wanted to look at the Bible since my wife died, but somehow this morning was different. I felt …well…I felt if I would just read it, I'd find some answers."

"Where did you read?" Ellen asked

"It was in the Psalms. I think it was Psalms ninety-one. I read the entire chapter, but as I read, well, it's hard to explain, but it seemed as if some of the verses jumped out at me. It was as if God was telling me to just trust Him, that He will take care of us all, including Abby, if we only trust Him."

Mary, sitting in the back seat, caught her breath and leaned forward, "Oh, Tony, I read the same chapter!" Her blue eyes were large with wonder.

Ellen covered her face with her hand, "Oh, this is no coincidence," she laughed. "I think God is really trying to get our attention. It's time we started leaning on God instead of our own understanding."

"The chapter was filled with promise," Tony added. "Do you remember, Mary? The verse talked about delivering us from our enemies. No matter where Abby is, I think God wants us to know that He will deliver her."

"I agree with both of you," Ellen nodded, "but I'd still like to talk to Phoebe about this. Do you mind Mary?"

"I don't mind at all. Actually, I have a lot of questions I'd like to ask her too."

The three were silent as they headed toward the bookstore, each deep in thought and amazed at the strange coincidence of Tony and Mary opening the Bible and reading the same passage when they each could have read in more than a thousand different places.

Chapter Twenty-Eight

Judy Sands walked to the window and pulled back the curtain. She was sure she heard a car, but it was only the mail carrier. Sighing, she went back into the kitchen and poured herself a third cup of coffee. The two little girls were chattering and giggling in the next room, engrossed in playing dress up.

Judy had checked on them moments before and marveled at how well they played together. They were having a tea party and laughed in uninhibited glee as they preened before the mirror in plastic jewelry, old hats, and gloves.

Where are those three? Where could they be? They said they'd only be gone about an hour, and here it is, already 3:30.

Restless and angry, Judy walked to the end of the driveway to get the mail. *A letter from my sister, Ruth, the utility bill, and what is this? I guess it's an advertisement for that new restaurant in town.* She threw the other letters on Tony's desk and sat down at the table to read her sister's letter.

Happy news about Ruth's grandchildren and a trip to Alaska to celebrate her forty-fifth wedding anniversary did little to take Judy's mind off what was happening in her life.

She sighed again. *Ruth's life seems so perfect compared to mine. Of course, she didn't lose her husband at sixty-five. She doesn't have to worry about money. She doesn't have to get up and go to work every day like I do. Most people my age are retired. Her daughter-in-law wasn't killed by a drunk driver. And she doesn't have a son who seems to be turning his back on everything I've ever taught him for a twit of a girl whose friends run off in the middle of the night for no good reason.*

The pity party was escalating as Judy dropped the letter from her sister in the waste basket. *Maybe I should bake something,* she thought. *That usually helps me take my mind off my worries.*

The ringing phone startled her out of her reverie, but she smiled in relief at the sound of her son's voice. "Thank God, Tony, where have you been? I was worried sick. Why didn't you call me?"

"I'm sorry, Mom. We're at the Morning Star Bookstore. We came here to talk to a friend of Ellen's, and the time just got away from us. How are the girls doing? It looks like we might be here a bit longer."

Judy was too angry to speak.

"Mom? Are you still there?"

165

"Yes, the girls are fine. I fed them lunch when you were still not back at one o'clock," she sniffed angrily.

"Well, I just called so you wouldn't worry."

"It's a little late for that."

"I'm sorry, Mom. Ellen was so upset, and Phoebe was helping her. I guess we just weren't thinking about the time."

"Phoebe Brown? Isn't she the woman with the Bible study?"

"Actually, yes, she also owns the Christian book store here in town."

For a reply, Judy offered more silence.

"If it's okay, I'd like to ask Ellen and Mary Catherine to stay for supper. It doesn't have to be anything special. I can just pick up something for sandwiches on the way home and maybe a bag of chips to make it easy if..."

"Tony, I have a headache, and I don't think tonight is a very good time for me to be entertaining company...maybe some other time."

"Okay, I'll be home in about twenty minutes or so."

Judy hung up the phone without saying goodbye. If she hadn't had a headache before, she certainly had one now. As she dialed the phone, hot tears welled in her eyes. Ring...ring...ring..., there was no answer. "Evelyn, where are you?" she whispered.

166

Who else can I call? I need to talk to someone. Lois? Maybe Lois can give me some perspective. At least she can tell me more about Ellen and maybe why this Phoebe person has such a hold on these young people.

Judy's hands shook as she dialed the phone. "Lois? Are you busy? I just made some fresh coffee, and I have some chocolate cupcakes about ready to come out of the oven. Can I bribe you to come over for a few minutes? I'm having…kind of…well, a little problem, and I need your advice."

Lois entered Judy's kitchen apprehensively, hoping this wasn't another ploy to try and convert her or make her feel guilty for not going to church. Despite her better judgment, her curiosity had drawn her across the street.

Motioning for Lois to sit down, Judy came straight to the point. "Tell me what you know about Ellen."

"Well, let's see, she's kind and fun, and it's evident she struggles with her weight. She is a little chubby but, of course, on her it looks good. Let's see, she works at the bridal shop and…"

"I know the surface stuff," Judy said in disgust. "What is she really like?"

Lois looked confused, and then a light went on and she laughed, "Ohhhh…do you mean does she have her cup set for Tony?"

167

Judy ignored the lighthearted reply and found herself confiding more than she'd intended. "Lois, I'm so worried. I'm afraid Tony's making some serious life mistakes."

"Do you mean they're sleeping together?"

Judy frowned, "No, it hasn't come to that…I don't think so anyway. It's just that Tony has become so, well, so irresponsible!"

"He's not going to work?"

Judy sighed exasperated, "No, it's not anything like that, it's just that Ellen has him going to this strange Bible study and, well, I'm just very concerned about where this could be leading. I think it might be a cult. I've tried to warn Tony, but this woman seems to have him mesmerized. She has him jumping through hoops to please her."

Lois was getting very nervous and started to reach in her purse for a cigarette but then remembered she was in a 'no smoking zone'. "I thought you Christians were all about the Bible. What could be wrong with going to a place where they read it."

Beginning to realize her mistake in confiding in Lois, Judy was even more exasperated. It was evident Lois couldn't possibly understand her worry, and it became even more evident when Lois began to scold her.

"Listen, Judy, I don't know much about Ellen, but if you brought me over here to talk against her, well, I'm afraid you have the wrong person. I'm not going to gossip about her. She's always been nice to me and not just me. Ellen is kind and compassionate to everyone. This religion thing isn't just some game she plays. She really lives what she believes. I've seen Joan practically spit in her face, and then Ellen will turn around and do something nice for her. She's genuinely concerned that something bad has happened to Abby. I think she's overreacting, but the girl is as true blue as they come. If Tony does end up with her, you should be glad. He's a grown man, Judy, let him be one. Don't you want him to be happy?"

Judy could feel the blood rushing to her face. *How could I have ever thought an unbeliever, a pagan like Lois, could understand what I was going through?*

Just as Judy was trying to come back with a reply, the kitchen door opened and in came Tony, Ellen, and Mary Catherine. The two little girls, hearing their parents' entrance, ran in with squeals of delight.

Tony explained they were all going for hamburgers and he was sorry his mom didn't feel well. A flurry of activity and the children had their shoes back on, their hair combed, and everyone but Judy was heading out the door.

Pale and distraught, Judy excused herself, made her way to her bedroom, closed the blinds, and lay down on the bed. "Dear God," she prayed, "dear God, help me. I have made a mess of everything, and I don't know how to fix it. I've tried so hard to be a Christian witness to Lois, and now she sees Ellen as the real Christian and me as a hypocritical gossip. Maybe I am, God. I don't even know anymore. I just know I'm miserable. Please, help me!"

Judy cried herself to sleep, but God saw her heart. The softening had begun.

Chapter Twenty-Nine

The sound of the doorbell startled Evelyn Wind out of deep sleep. It was too early for visitors, and she wondered who in the world it could be. Grabbing her robe, she staggered half asleep to the front door and opened it to a very distraught Judy Sands.

"Oh, Evelyn, I'm so glad you're home! Where's Pastor Wind?"

Evelyn tried to gather her thoughts, but she was still a little foggy from the sleeping pill she'd taken the night before.

"I, ah, well…let's see. He said he was getting up early this morning to play golf."

Judy sat at the kitchen table without an invitation as Evelyn ran water for coffee. Taking a tissue out of her purse, Judy blew her nose loudly. Her eyes were red and swollen, giving evidence of a sleepless night and much weeping.

"Did you notice that Tony and Jennifer were not at church with me yesterday?"

Evelyn was trying to keep her composure but was finding it difficult. *The phone calls were bad enough, but now this. What is wrong with this woman? Monday is the only day my husband has off and she comes barging in here, expecting him, expecting me to be at her beck and call when it's barely daylight!* Evelyn squinted at the clock, 6:30. *Surely she wouldn't stay long, she'd be late for work.* Evelyn wanted to lash out at the woman, but she forced herself to pour two cups of coffee, sit down, and ask her as kindly as she could muster what the problem was. "Now, please tell me what's happening?"

"I couldn't go to work today. I called in and I am taking the day off. I'm just too upset to concentrate."

Oh, great, this could become an all-day marathon of self-pity! Evelyn thought, but she disciplined herself to look concerned, in case there really was a problem, and said, "Just start at the beginning, Judy."

"Well, it's hard to know where the beginning is. As you know, Tony and Jennifer have had a really hard year, with the accident and everything. Our life has been hell for the last three years. First, my precious Stanley dying, and then...and then...," Judy began to sob.

Evelyn could feel compassion growing inside of her. She silently asked God to forgive her for being self-centered and took Judy's hand. "I'm so sorry, Judy. I know you and Tony have been through it, and I won't pretend to know how you feel. I'm sure it has been terrible."

"Tony was so close to his father, and then to lose his wife too! I think something inside of him just snapped!"

"Whatever do you mean?" Evelyn cocked her head, trying to understand.

"Well...for one thing, he's been mesmerized by that girl across the street, that Ellen person, and now he has been running around with Mary Catherine from my office. You know, she's pregnant, and who knows who the father is? Maybe that's why her husband left her!"

Evelyn could feel her compassion quickly dissipating as Judy's conversation took on a gossipy hue. Unconsciously she pulled back.

Judy continued, "You know I've been witnessing to Mary Catherine, and she was even going to church with us and bringing that sweet little girl. I never thought in my wildest dreams that Tony would get involved with someone like her, you know, divorced and pregnant and all. I'm not even sure she is divorced, and here he is running around with her. What if people think the child is his?"

"Calm down, Judy. I'm sure anyone who knows Tony realizes he is just being a friend.

173

Besides, I thought you told me he was interested in Ellen?"

"That's just it. I have no idea what he's up to. He puts his arm around first one and then the other. On top of that, they all went out of town yesterday to visit Ellen's mother. Ellen claims to be a Christian and here she is dragging Tony, those two babies, and Mary Catherine halfway across the state when they should be in church!"

"Maybe they went to church with Ellen's mother."

"That's another thing! What kind of a church? Remember when I told you about Phoebe Brown? She and her husband are filling these young people with all kinds of strange doctrines. Tony told me he felt the presence of God! *Presence*! What do you think that means? It sounds spooky to me. You can't feel God! What's wrong with him? He told me he could *feel* God! Next thing I know, he will tell me he hears God speaking to him! I tell you, it is frightening to say the least. I'm afraid he is involved with a bunch of Holy Rollers. Why, it's probably a cult." She took a sip of coffee and tried to compose herself. "Then he told me he cried out to God to change him, to make him a brand new person, and he said God did! He said he could feel God's love wrap around him like a physical force, and it gave him so much joy that he wanted to sing and dance! *Dance*, Evelyn! Can you believe he said God made him want to dance?"

Evelyn's eyebrows knit together in concentration. "Well, David in the Bible danced before the Lord when the Holy Spirit filled him with joy. Maybe that's not as strange as one would think," she said thoughtfully. "And Judy, don't you think it was just a figure of speech?"

"That's not all. He said he wants to see other people change the way he was changed. He said he wanted to see," she took a gulping breath, "that I am changed!" She began to sob. "He said God wanted to heal my broken heart! He came right out and said it wasn't right for us to continue grieving the way we were. He said the Bible talks about grief remaining for a while, but joy comes in the morning. He said Dad and Carol are in heaven, and God wants to fill us with His joy. Why, he even said grief can become an addiction, and that God wants to heal our broken hearts. He even said neither of us would ever heal until we started praising God that our loved ones were in heaven. It was almost like he was trying to tell me to be glad that we both lost our mates!"

"Oh, surely he didn't mean it that way, although there is a verse that tells us to rejoice in tribulation. Maybe that's what he meant."

Judy looked at her in astonishment. This conversation was certainly not going in the direction she had hoped for. "Evelyn, he inferred that I just cry all the time because I get some kind of pleasure out of mourning."

"Surely not, I'm sure he didn't mean that. What did you say?"

"Well, I gave him a piece of my mind, of course. I told him I could never, ever forget my precious Stanley and that he should be ashamed of himself for talking that way about the two most precious people in the world."

"And?"

"He told me that, of course, he would never forget his love for his father or his wife, but if we allow God to heal our broken hearts, that in time we can be free of the excruciating pain and only recall the precious memories. Can you believe he would talk to me like that? That he would speak so disrespectfully of his wife and his father to his mother?"

Evelyn raised her eyebrows again but said nothing. Grimacing in pain, Evelyn got up to refill the coffee cups and tried to think of the best way to encourage Judy and send her on her way. Sliding the tissue box toward her she said, "Judy, what if you and I go to that Bible study at the Browns? We can check it out and find out if what they are teaching is false doctrine. We'll take notes and I'm sure Don will help us figure out a way to combat anything that is anti-God or anti-Bible or anti-church."

"You would do that for me?"

"Yes, I think it's the best thing we can do under the circumstances. Besides, I have to admit I'm a little curious. I remember hearing my grandfather talk about meetings like this that happened around the turn of the century. People humbled themselves and repented and all kinds of amazing things happened, outside of church as well as in. Wouldn't it be incredible if what Tony says is true and there really is a move of God?"

Judy missed the 'might be true' part and seemed relieved that Evelyn would make this sacrifice for her. "Oh, thank you, Evelyn! You are such a good friend…but…aren't you afraid to go there?"

"Pshaw, how could it hurt an old bird like me?"

Leaving Evelyn's kitchen, Judy had a renewed hope thinking, *We will get to the bottom of this once and for all. Tony has always been a reasonable person. He has always respected Pastor. Once he sees the truth, he will give up that little harlot that's trying to seduce him and soon this will be over.*

After Judy left, Evelyn sat at the table nursing her cup of coffee until it was cold. Remembering how her grandfather used to talk about the healings

177

he had seen sent her mind reeling. *Perhaps, who could tell? Judy says they pray for the sick. What if sometimes, at least once in a while, God does still do a miracle? Oh God, if it is possible, please let it happen to me.*

Chapter Thirty

Joan lay beside her husband trying to sort through everything that had happened. The yacht rocked peacefully in the harbor. The gulls called to each other in the background, blending their cries with Peter's soft snoring. The early morning light broke through the porthole causing the reflection of water and light to dance on the wall in a delightful and playful pattern.

I should be the happiest girl in the world, she thought as she moved her body closer to Peter's. It would do no good. Even in his sleep, his resolve to have no intimacy with her was apparent.

The beautiful wedding had been clouded by memories of what Katrina called the real wedding. All night long Joan was tormented by nightmares of her wedding dress full of holes, tattered and torn, dirty rags barely covering her body as she carried dead roses and walked toward her handsome lover who morphed into an ugly creature, drool mixed with blood dripping from his mouth.

Her sister Charlotte said the wedding was magnificent. The bridesmaids, all friends of Peter, wore ice-blue gowns, and each girl was perfectly attired and groomed down to the last detail. Joan's gown was, of course, the most expensive in the bridal shop, and flowers filled the church in such abundance that some said it was like walking into Paradise.

Charlotte, Lois, Katrina, and the servants who would soon serve Joan, were the only ones sitting on the bride's side, but that made no difference to Joan. Saying her parents were much too sick and old to travel produced the sympathy she had hoped for. Explaining she was new in town and was too busy to make friends satisfied Peter's family.

Flashbacks of what Katrina called the real ceremony crowded out the beauty of the church wedding. In her mind's eye, she saw the marble altar. The drugs had softened everything at the time, but somehow her subconscious would not leave it alone. When she least expected it, she would once again see the fireplace, or was it a firepit, with a monstrous idol of some kind officiating? At first, everyone bowed prostrate before the idol, and then Katrina, chanting, led them in a dance of some sort. Next, she instructed Joan to lie on the altar and welcome the union of herself and the being they worshipped. The chanting stopped as the fire turned blue and exploded toward the vaulted ceiling. Joan vaguely remembered wondering how the room could be so big under the modest farmhouse. *Evidently, the house was built over a large underground cave.*

Lying beside her husband, she tried to sort out what was real and what was a dream. She remembered people standing in a circle, worshiping her and calling her the chosen one. Haunted day and night by the experience, she tried to block it out of her mind and concentrate on her new wealth and position, but the monstrous dream refused to fade.

Trembling, she once again mused, *I remember lying on that stone altar. Why is everything so hazy? Of course, I must have been drugged. I do remember Katrina screaming, "Today, on June twenty-first, in the year of nineteen fifty-nine, Joan Newel becomes the mother of our savior. We now call on the god of this world to impregnate Joan. Come, Lucifer. You who have been known by many names through the thousands of years, we worship you and call you forth now. Come and impregnate our daughter, come and take human form. We have waited for this day. You are the one destined to take your place as a mighty leader in the future. Your reign will then begin, and you will receive the worship and adoration that is rightfully yours. Come forth, child of destiny."*

Joan recalled floating in and out of consciousness, hearing loud music and beating drums, and blurry forms of bodies whirling about her. But then the blackness would take over again.

Peter rolled over and playfully ruffled her hair. "Hey."

"I've been awake." *Awake and trying to make sense of this insanity,* she thought.

"Why the sour face? I'm taking you shopping this morning! This island is known for its beautiful jewelry and..."

"Peter, I don't want jewelry, I want you!"

"Soon enough," he said, taking both of her hands in his and kissing them. We will take you to the doctor right after the honeymoon and establish your pregnancy. As soon as that happens, we will be just like every other young married couple."

"But what if..."

"Then we will have another ceremony. If you are not pregnant, we may have to prove our sincerity and willingness to obey." He looked into her eyes as he continued to hold her hands tightly.

She wanted to wrench her hands out of his and leap from the bed. She wanted to run, to escape, but his eyes held her mesmerized and she could not move.

"You told us you are willing to have Lucifer's child. We had the ceremony, but if for some reason you did not become pregnant, we may have to choose another sacrifice," he whispered as he continued to kiss the palms of her hands.

Terror enveloped her as she realized what he was saying. Her heart was pounding in her throat and she gulped. "Peter, I can't."

"It is your destiny. We must cooperate with him. He has given you every worldly pleasure, now we must prove to him we are completely surrendered."

Sitting in the center of the bed, she tried to pull her hands away, but he held them tightly. She finally broke his gaze and looked at the floor.

"I can't...physically hurt anyone. I'm willing to carry Lucifer's child, but I can't...can't hurt anyone."

"You only have to choose her, Joan. If more is required of you, we will help you. You will be given strength when the time comes. If he demands the sacrifice of an innocent one, of a virgin child, it will be your duty to cooperate."

"All right, yes, okay, if...it comes to that...if I have to."

He dropped her hands, and she slid from him. Trying to keep her voice light, she said she would shower now and get ready for the day.

As the water beat on her body, her mind was racing. *Somehow, I must conceive a child before this trip is over...somehow! These people are maniacs... they are insane, I can't let their insanity invade my mind. I must find a way to get away from Peter for a while. Somewhere on this island, there is someone who will gladly take me to his bed. It's the right time of the month so all I need is a willing partner. Once I'm pregnant, I don't care what happens. This is just a crazy game they play. Rich people get bored. Peter will tire of all of this soon, and I will have everything.*

She leaned against the shower stall gagging. Dry heaves wracked her body as the water beat on her. *I'm sick to my stomach half of every day. Maybe I'm already pregnant, but I can't take the chance.* She staggered to turn the knobs off and wrapped a huge fluffy white towel around her. *I'll be alright, I'll be alright. Yes...maybe I'm already pregnant. Maybe this constant nausea is morning sickness. Oh, who am I trying to fool,* she groaned. *Whatever I do, Katrina will know. She probably knows what I'm thinking this very moment, but I've got to risk it. I can't...I refuse...I will not be responsible for another child's death.*

Thirty-One

Mayor Hamilton sat at his desk, his head in his hands. Sergeant Grant stood before him. The mayor sighed, motioned for Larry to close the door, and told him to pull up a chair.

"So, Larry, you have the girl locked in the bomb shelter of the old Cramer Building. What next?"

"Well, I'd like to move her. For one thing, old lady Kelly said she found her screaming her lungs out."

"There's not much chance of anyone hearing her. Those walls are two feet thick. When Hollis Cramer built that building, he had just come back from fighting in World War I. He was sure America would be involved in another world war one day and..."

"Spare me the history," Larry interrupted. "I just don't like the idea of her down there while Marilyn Musgrave conducts business as usual above in the bridal shop."

Calvin Hamilton stood and walked to the window. "I wish I'd never gotten involved in this mess. Why didn't you just arrest Polworth six months ago when you first suspected they might be a satanic coven? You could have gotten her on possession, at least."

"Yes, and she would have been out in twenty-four hours, and we still wouldn't have enough evidence to stop the child trafficking."

"We can't risk another child."

Larry took a deep breath and let it out slowly, "Do you think I don't beat myself up every day over that Harrison child? I'm sick about it, but Katrina still doesn't trust me enough to let me attend her meetings. This has not been easy, Sir. She indeed manipulates people with drugs and hypnosis, but she also has genuine powers that…"

"Calm down, surely you don't believe in that hocus pocus."

"I wish to God I didn't, but I do. Some things can't be explained. I have a praying mom and she says this is not something to be taken lightly. It's a battle between good and evil. These people look like proper upstanding citizens, but for their success, they have sold their souls to the devil."

Larry got up and began to pace. "Mayor, you and I have gone to the same church since I was a little kid."

"Yes, I remember you as a toe-headed altar boy when Wilma and I first were married. What does that have to do with any of this?"

"Just this, we both know our church attendance has often been more social than spiritual."

The mayor replied with a "humph," neither denying nor affirming.

"Lately, I've begun to realize I want more, need more, just to make it in this world. I'm only thirty years old and I've already seen more evil than I've ever dreamed possible. My mom's been praying for me for a long time, but it wasn't until I started working on this case that I realized what she was talking about. I've just started to understand that without prayer, without God giving us the ability to fight this evil, we don't have a chance."

"Okay, okay, I don't need to hear about your mother, and I didn't call you in here to be preached at. Just make sure you get enough evidence to put these lunatics away forever."

"That's the goal."

"What if they suspect you?"

"Believe me, if they did, I wouldn't be here to tell you about it."

"I want this thing stopped. You're sure they think Abigail McDonald is dead?"

"Yes, I convinced Musgrave that I took care of it. We're checking on Abby at two every morning. We take her food and care for her personal needs. Elizabeth Kelly has worked for my mom for years, and her son, Wallace, is a little simple but as honest and trustworthy as she is. I told him to take a rifle in case someone from the organization tried to interfere."

"A rifle? That doesn't sound very smart. You're letting this man, who you admit isn't the sharpest crayon in the box, prance around with a rifle?"

"As far as I can tell, these people don't operate with firearms. If they're seen, I told Mrs. Kelly to say they were shooting rats. They never enter the bridal shop. There's a cellar door that leads to the underground entrance. I doubt even those who once knew about it remember it's there. Mrs. Kelly's son works as Musgrave's groundkeeper, so if they run into her, he has a valid right to be there."

The mayor sighed and leaned back in his chair, staring at the ceiling. "Larry, when you first came to me with this story, I honestly thought you had lost your marbles."

"At times I've wondered about that myself, but that night I offered to give Richard Thorton a ride home because he was too drunk to drive…"

"I know, I know, because he was too drunk to drive," the mayor said, waving the story aside. "I still don't understand why you didn't bring him in when he started talking."

"I told you, he passed out. When he sobered up, he denied everything, and besides, he had just said fragments of thoughts. He never said anything concrete, and yet I knew what he meant and what he did say caused me to realize they only meant to drug the child but gave her too great a dose of barbiturates."

"I still don't understand why you didn't bring him in."

"Because I had so little evidence. I had to piece together the few words he spoke in a drunken stupor. As I said, he passed out on me. When he came to, he denied saying anything and then the next night, before I could bring him in for questioning, he was killed in that terrible accident."

"Well, we know his brakes were cut, but we have no evidence it was one of Katrina's people," the mayor sighed.

"I'm sure it was one of Katrina's followers, but how can we ever prove it?"

"Back to Abigail MacDonald, what are you going to do with her? We can't hold her hostage forever. She's the innocent one in all of this."

"Yes, I know," Sargent Grant sighed. "Do you think we should move her? I told Mrs. Kelly to try and reassure her, to explain she was being protected."

"I guess you better leave well enough alone, although I can't believe you stashed her right under Musgrave's nose."

"It was the only thing I could think of at the time. It all happened so fast. Once I realized she was probably just knocked out and would be okay, I told the women to leave, and I'd take care of it. Then I remembered playing in that old basement when I was a little kid and accidentally coming across the bomb shelter. It's located a full level below the basement."

"What did you do with her car?"

"I drove it to my mother's and hid it in her garage right after I put Abby in the bomb shelter. My mom drove me back to the store to pick up my squad car. That poor girl is probably scared silly, but we can't take a chance that she'll be seen by any of that group and blow my cover. I guess it's safer to leave her where she is, for now anyway."

"What about those people who are looking for her, those friends of hers? Do you think they're going to make trouble?"

"I know they're worried, but at the present, they're not a priority. Too much is at stake for me to be concerned about their peace of mind."

The mayor stood and dismissed Larry. "Sergeant, I expect you to wind this up soon. Soon! Do you hear? If they take one more child…"

"It won't happen, Sir. I have more than you to answer to. And...," he hesitated a moment not sure how much he could say without looking like a religious nut but continued, "Sir, God won't let it happen again."

Mayor Hamilton looked into Larry's eyes, holding his gaze for a moment. "I hope that's right. If it's not...," he spoke barely above a whisper, "God help us all."

Larry walked out of the courthouse with the weight of the conversation bearing down on him. Mom, Trudy, and Aunt Alice had prayed with him in the afternoon. He couldn't tell them much, just that it involved the missing children. His mom was trying to persuade him to attend one of Brown's Bible studies, but he wasn't sure he was ready for that. Besides, there was no way he was going to jeopardize this case, let alone his life, by being seen with Christians.

He prayed silently as he made his way toward the car. *Lord, Aunt Alice says you have given Christians authority over demons and principalities of evil. Father, I know I don't know you as well as I should, but I am a believer. I do belong to you. If my mother is right and we Christians have been too wishy-washy to use our authority against evil, please forgive us. This is so new to me, God, I don't know how much I believe. Sometimes it seems it's as strange as Polworth. All I know is when these ladies pray, they seem to get results. Please, God, show me how to win. If I can glean from the few slurred words Thorton said, that the Harrison child is the first one they killed and that was by accident, if that's so, God, where are the other children? Please, God, help me to find them and please, God, stop every plan to take more children.*

He got in the car, closed the door, and in the privacy of his squad car, he cried, "In the name of Jesus, I take authority over all of the demon forces that are behind the abduction of these children. I loose the truth to be made known and lies to have no power." He felt a little silly, but at the same time, he could feel faith beginning to grow inside of him. "Thank you, God," he whispered. "Thank you for hearing my prayer."

Chapter Thirty-Two

The sky was a strange yellow-green as Mary Catherine pulled up in front of Phoebe Brown's bookstore. She hurriedly made her way into the shop, anxiously glancing toward the sky as big fat droplets of rain began to fall.

A tiny bell over the door announced her arrival. Phoebe came from the back of the store, a bucket in one hand and a mop in the other. "Leak," she said with a big smile. Mary looked back toward the large glass window as a peal of thunder made it rattle.

"It looks like another bad storm. Isn't this the strangest weather? Sorry about your leak," she said all in one breath.

"If it ever stops raining, my husband can fix the roof. Until then…," she held up the bucket as an explanation. "But I'm sure you didn't come here to talk about my leak. Is there any word on Abby?"

"No, and it's really hard to stay in faith. Her mother calls me every day. It's difficult to keep her spirits up when I can't even stay in faith myself. I keep telling her we are trusting God, but I'm sure she thinks that's pretty lame."

"Ellen told me you had trouble finding a contact number for Abby's mom. How did you find her?"

"Lois had the number all along. Her aunt owns the house that the girls all rent, and she has them provide emergency contact information when they sign the lease."

"How are you feeling, Mary? You look tired."

"Pretty good, actually. The doctor has moved up my due date."

As sheets of rain pelted the window, Phoebe suggested they have a cup of tea. Mary followed her to the back room and pulled up a chair as Phoebe turned on the electric plate under the tea kettle.

"Okay, you said on the phone you needed to talk, but it's not about Abby?"

"Well, I guess it really is in a way. I've prayed and prayed for her, but sometimes I wonder if God hears me. He seems so far away."

"Mary, remember the night you surrendered your life to God?"

"Yes."

"Don't forget that when you did, He came to live inside of you. He knows our every need even before we pray. We sometimes have the idea that He is far away in Heaven. We think we have to work ourselves into some kind of spiritual state before He can hear us, but that's not what the Bible says."

"I just read the scripture that says, 'Greater is He that is in you than he that is in the world,' but I guess I didn't make the connection that it meant God lives inside of me."

"Yes, and the 'he' that is in the world is God's enemy, the Devil. That's why the Devil hates us. You're learning how to walk by faith, Mary, and as you read the New Testament and you start doing what the Bible teaches, you'll grow stronger and stronger. Sometimes we have feelings that help us to believe God is with us and that He is right there to help us, but the real maturity comes when we don't have the feelings and we still believe."

"I think I understand. But if God knows everything I need, why do I have to pray? Won't he just give me what's best for me?"

"As you get to know God better, you'll see that God, through His Holy Spirit, never forces himself on anyone. Because He gave us free will, He waits for us to come to Him and ask for His help."

Mary Catherine nodded. After visiting for close to an hour, she suddenly realized her lunch break was over. "Wow, I need to run, but thank you so much. I've got so much to learn. But what we've talked about today has really helped me. Thanks for the tea and the good words. Oh, by the way, I've invited Judy Sands to Bible study next week, and she's coming."

"You invited Tony's mother?" Phoebe said in an amazed tone.

"Yes, you know we work together. She asked if she could bring her best friend, Evelyn."

"Evelyn Wind, the pastor's wife?" Phoebe whispered.

"Yes, isn't this great?"

"I…ah…well, yes, I guess so," Phoebe gulped nervously. "It's just that…"

"Yes?"

"Never mind, God's plans and purpose are higher than mine. This will be very interesting."

"Oh, before I leave, one other thing. I keep having this thought that somehow Abby's disappearance is linked to the missing children. Do you think this is just my imagination?"

"Many times this is the way God imparts information. It is unusual to hear an actual voice, but when God is speaking to us, it's more of a knowing. When this happens, the information is from the Holy Spirit. Sometimes when we are troubled about something and we take the time to quiet ourselves before the Lord, He imparts this knowing that everything is going to be alright. God is faithful to comfort us even when we're not sure of what's going on. Did you know the Holy Spirit is called our comforter?"

"Yes, I believe Phillip said something about that at the last Bible study, but it's different to hear it taught and to actually experience it."

"I hope this has helped you, Mary. I know you need to get back to work, but would you like me to pray before you go?"

Quickly glancing at her watch, Mary nodded, "Yes, I think it's important."

Phoebe bowed her head. "Father, we don't understand all that is happening, but you told us that where two or more are gathered in your name you are right here with us. We also know that even if one of us is praying alone, we are never truly alone because you are in us, so we always have at least two. Thank you, Father, for this assurance. Having established this, we pray in faith that the abductions will be stopped, that Abby will be found, and that every single missing child will be protected by your angels and returned to their parents. In Jesus' name we pray, amen."

Chapter Thirty-Three

Closing his sermon, Reverend Wind looked over his tiny congregation and was sure at least two of his elderly parishioners were asleep. As the rustic pipe organ pumped out a familiar hymn, he made his way to the back of the church.

Mary Catherine, Jill, Ellen, Tony, Judy and little Jen filled a pew near the back and were the first to leave. As they passed by, he had the uneasy feeling that the light grew dim at their departure.

He tried to concentrate on the mumbled compliments of the rest of the congregation as they filed past, but his mind kept returning to that row of shiny faces. It was almost as if a spotlight beamed on them, and now it was gone.

The church emptied, and he made his way to the platform. Studying the pew they had occupied, he chided himself. It now looked much the same as the other pews.

Evelyn was waiting, purse and Bible in hand. "What are you doing, Donald?" she called out in irritation. "My pot roast is drying out."

"I was just wondering about the lighting," he replied. "It seems so dark and dreary in here. I think perhaps a lightbulb has burned out, but I can't seem to find it."

She gave him a huge sigh that spoke her impatience more than words, and then her silent disapproval. As they were turning into the driveway, she began to mellow. "It was nice to see Tony back in church."

"Yes, and he brought his friends."

"See, I told you Tony has his head on straight. Judy is upset over nothing. Still, I did promise to go with her to that Bible study or prayer meeting or whatever it is that Tony's so involved in."

Reverend Wind blinked nervously. "You what? Evelyn, are you serious?"

"I said I would go. What's wrong with that?"

"Evelyn, you can't. What will people think? This town is small, and you know how people talk. If you go, it will be seen as an endorsement. I've…I've heard things about these people!"

"What kind of things?"

"Well…I don't know exactly…just that there is a lot of emotionalism and the people are duped into believing it is the presence of God."

Evelyn laughed scoffing.

"Evelyn, this isn't funny. We can pray for Tony to come to his senses without getting

199

involved. Going to that Bible study will give people the idea that I approve of that kind of thing!"

"Simmer down, Don. I thought it would help mend the fences between Judy and Tony. And look, I must be right, they were all at church today. Judy and I are just going to take notes so you can confront Tony and explain to him why he should stop going. Pshaw…I don't think there is one thing to fear."

He frowned at her, closed his eyes for a moment as if he were trying to come back with the right retort, and then surprised her by saying, "Alright, then I'm going with you!"

She looked at him in amazement, shrugged her shoulders, and went into the house to put dinner on the table.

Don lingered in the yard, not wanting to continue the conversation. *I wonder what has really happened to Tony. It's evident this Ellen person has caught his attention. She's a beautiful girl, but it's more than that. And what is going on with Mary Catherine? When she was here before, she was so despondent. Now she's glowing. I would say it was because of the child she carries, except she was so desperately unhappy the first time Judy brought her to church. I wonder what's made the difference.*

Feeling very old and tired, Donald Wind pondered the years. *How many weddings, funerals, and baptisms have I conducted in the last forty years? How many have I counseled? How many, if any, have I really helped? There was a time when I first entered the seminary, I was so thrilled to have the opportunity to help people that I could barely go to sleep at night. I was excited, no, I was honored just to do God's work. When did pastoring evolve into administration? When did I start dreading everything? Where did the time go?*

Sighing heavily, he entered the house. Evelyn was setting the table. "I hear Peter Ellington and his wife are back from their honeymoon," she said, trying to make light conversation. "They weren't in church today," she continued.

Donald picked up the newspaper and turned to the sports page. "I doubt we'll see much of those two," he mumbled. "Peter only came on holidays before he was married. His parents were always Christmas and Easter Christians."

"Still, perhaps you should visit them. She's such a pretty little thing."

"Perhaps I will," he answered, thinking *as if it would do any good.*

"So…you are going with us?"

"I think it would be best," he said, as he studied the sports page.

Evelyn looked at her husband over her glasses but didn't comment. *You can't fool me, Donald Wind. You're just as curious as I am.* She changed the subject as she set the steaming pot roast on the table. *This is going to be very interesting, very interesting indeed.* Something fluttered inside of her. She wasn't sure, but it felt like anticipation.

Chapter Thirty-Four

Judy Sands dried her hands on the dish towel as Tony put the last of the dishes away. He looked gleeful, chattering about how thrilled he was that both Pastor and Evelyn were coming to the Brown's Bible study tonight.

He wouldn't be so happy if he knew why they were coming, she thought. *Poor Tony, he's so deceived, but it's better to burst his balloon tonight before he goes any deeper into this apostasy.*

Trying to change the subject, she picked up the mail on the desk and exclaimed, "I forgot to tell you, we've won two dinners at that new Greek restaurant."

"Really?" he answered back, "That's great, but we better hurry Mom. I don't want to be late."

"Do you think the girls will be okay with Lois?" she asked.

"I'm sure they will be fine, Mom...we won't be gone that long."

"I told Evelyn we'd wait for them outside. Is that okay with you?"

"Of course," Tony answered, "we want them to feel welcome. It will probably feel less awkward if we all walk in together."

~~~

Across town, Mary Catherine tried to hurry supper, go through the mail, and answer Jill's excited questions about Lois and Jennifer. A letter with a bright red border grabbed her attention. "You Won!" it announced.

Not counting the jellybeans she had counted correctly at the fifth-grade carnival, this was the only prize Mary Catherine had ever won. She read the letter again and smiled. *Dinner for two at the finest Greek restaurant in Northern Indiana. Come, bring a friend, and enjoy Apollyno's Den. This prize can only be claimed by the person named above and has a monetary value of fifty dollars. It cannot be redeemed for cash. We know you will enjoy our large selection of Greek Cuisine. Thank you for submitting your name in our May drawing.*

Mary looked at the letter, puzzled. *I don't remember entering my name in a contest. I guess someone else entered for me; how nice. Now who should I ask,* she wondered. Placing the letter under a magnet on the refrigerator, she turned up the flame on Jill's dinner. Lois had volunteered to babysit again, and Mary was looking forward to the Bible study.

Just as she started to clear the table, the doorbell announced Lois was there. Moments later, the two little girls made their way to Jill's bedroom while Lois motioned for Mary to scurry out, saying she would be happy to clear the table.

Sliding into the back seat, Mary Cathrine was greeted by a very serious Judy while in the front. Tony and Ellen were all smiles.

"You'll never guess what just happened to me!" Mary announced. "I've just won two tickets to that new Greek restaurant, Apollyon's Den! I'm not sure how I feel about Greek food," she laughed, "but it's a free meal!"

"We received the same letter," Judy and Tony crowed. All four laughed, and the atmosphere seemed to be less strained as they discussed the possibility of the four of them going to lunch after church next Sunday.

They arrived at the Bible study much too quickly for Judy. She got out of the car hesitantly but felt her courage return as Evelyn and Pastor pulled up behind them. The three visitors were trying their best to return the friendly overtures as they were seated on folding chairs toward the back.

A man, a little younger than Tony, came over to shake hands. "Pastor, how wonderful to see you here!" he said.

Don gulped and swallowed nervously as he held out his hand. He could hardly believe his eyes. It was Raymond Harrison, and he looked so…so…happy!

Across the room was Jenna, her dark curly hair bobbing enthusiastically as she agreed with the two young women she was talking to. *Both of them seem to have that same shine…glow…what is it…? Whatever it is, it's what I saw on Tony, Ellen, and Mary Catherine last Sunday. How can this be? I just buried their child…how long has it been…less than a month ago? Where is the grief, the anger, the unbearable depression? It seems to be gone…but why and how?*

Realizing his wife was intent on talking to Judy and may not have noticed, he sat down and took Evelyn's hand. Searching her face for an answer, he whispered, "The Harrisons are here."

She nodded, "Yes, I saw." He could tell she was just as bewildered as he was.

As everyone began to settle, Phoebe Brown stepped to the microphone. "If everyone can find a seat, we have a wonderful surprise for you. Jenna and Raymond Harrison have agreed to share their testimonies with us."

After a short prayer, Philip handed the microphone to Raymond.

Chapter Thirty-Five

As Raymond stepped to the front, a hush fell over the little group. "I guess everyone here knows the story of how we lost our daughter."

Pastor Wind leaned forward in his chair. He loved this man. He had baptized him as a baby and baptized Brenda too. He could feel the pain of their loss wash over him.

"Before we lost Brenda, I guess, truthfully, I didn't think very much about God. My wife and I went to church on Sunday, we gave money to the church, and we tried to just be good people. I guess I figured since we'd been baptized, we'd done our duty," he paused, "I…I guess we just thought God wasn't too interested in us on a personal level and honestly, I guess we weren't too interested in Him either. When Brenda disappeared, that all changed. We started praying like we'd never prayed before. We were desperate and, of course, we didn't know she was already gone." His voice broke. "We…we didn't know she was already with Jesus, and then, well…when they found her…I just didn't think I could stand it. I just didn't want to live anymore. I was furious with God, and I just didn't want anything to do with Him. All I could think was who could trust or believe in a God who would let that happen to an innocent little child."

Judy Sands stared at the floor. *Why are they putting Raymond through this agony? Hasn't the poor boy suffered enough?* She could feel her anger growing as the memory of losing Carol was still fresh. Listening to Raymond, she moved from the Harrison's grief back into her own. It was hard to listen as a flood of memories engulfed her. Looking up, she felt as if she must have missed some of what was being said because Raymond was smiling as he continued.

"Last week, Tony Sands came to visit us. He said, 'God loved us,' and to tell you the truth, that infuriated me." Raymond smiled at Tony, "Sorry guy."

Tony smiled and waved his hand in dismissal.

"Then Tony said something that no one else was saying. He told us it wasn't God's will for Brenda to die. Everyone else was talking like God wanted Brenda to be with him…and that God needed a little angel. I didn't see how I could trust a God that would be that heartless…a God that would let some monster kill and mutilate her just so he could have her up in heaven."

Pastor Wind stared at his hands. He knew he had been the one who had told them that God's ways were higher than man's ways and that God allowed Brenda to die to make them stronger.

Raymond continued. "Tony explained to us that there is a real Devil and that his main goal was to make God look bad by destroying lives and causing people to believe that all the tragedy in the world is God's will. He showed me a lot of Bible verses that proved God only wants good for his people. Verses like John 10:10, The thief cometh not, but for to steal, and to kill, and destroy; but Jesus said, 'I have come that they might have life, and that they might have it more abundantly.'

"Tony said Satan was the thief in this verse, and as Tony began to explain things, I realized I didn't know God at all. I never read the Bible because I thought it was mainly for theologians, pastors, or people like that. I can't explain how the breakthrough came, but little by little, I saw that God really is on my side. He didn't take Brenda away from us. God wanted us happy, not devastated. I also realized that the Devil wanted us to hate God. I began to think that maybe I could trust God after all. You can't trust someone unless you know they want good things for you. Well...I guess that's all. Jenna, do you have something to add?"

Jenna took the microphone. Her hand was shaking, but her voice was strong. "When Raymond first told me that Tony wanted to come by and talk to us about what happened," she laughed nervously, "I said no. It seemed like everyone wanted to go over and over all of the details. I just couldn't take it anymore. But then, well, I guess God was softening my heart. I was looking for answers, so I relented.

"At first, Tony just sat and listened. When he finally started talking, I knew somehow that what he had to say would be different. For one thing, he had recently lost someone he loved too. I knew losing Carol was not Tony's fault, and that he could understand how unfair our loss was. It was a puzzle to me. How could he be free of the anger when anger was consuming me? I told him I knew he loved Carol, and I asked him how he could possibly forgive the drunk driver who ran her off the road."

"He got my attention when he said he couldn't. Then he explained to Ray and me that God gave man jurisdiction over the world back in the Garden of Eden. When man sinned, he handed that jurisdiction over to Satan. I always thought God was in control of everything that happened in the world. Tony showed me in the Bible that Satan is the god of this world. He said because we have free will, God won't cross our will, but He does have control in the situations where we purposely give Him control. The way we take control away from Satan is by surrendering our lives to God and by praying that God's will is done. It doesn't mean that as Christians we will never have anything bad happen in our lives. On the contrary, sometimes it feels as if our battle is so strong against evil that we don't know how we will survive. Realizing that in this battle against evil we have God right there to strengthen us helps us to endure. There will always be trials in our lives, but God will carry us through every storm.

"I guess that's when I realized that I've never understood what being a Christian is all about. I didn't want to go to hell so when I married Ray, I joined the church and was baptized. I've always tried to be good and do what was kind. I didn't realize God wanted a relationship with me, or that as a Christian I was in partnership with God in a war against evil. Somehow, I missed the point that I could pray and trust God with my life. After talking to Tony, I knew I wanted to change, that I wanted to give control of my life to God. I wanted Him to be Lord over every area of my life, not just save me from hell. I began to realize that although there will still be bad things happening in the world, and even to me personally, I can trust God to use even the bad things for my good.

"Then I knew I had a decision to make. When I asked God to forgive me for blaming Him for all the bad things that were happening to us, something wonderful happened. I felt like a heavy coat, almost like something I was wearing, was lifted off me.

The next thing that happened changed everything. I suddenly knew Brenda wasn't in my past, Brenda was in my glorious future. I could feel God's healing power filling me, changing me, and I knew I didn't have to hang on to the pain any longer. Hanging on to the pain didn't honor Brenda or prove I loved her. Yes, I loved my daughter with all my heart, and I still love her, but I can honor her more by releasing the pain and trusting God than by remaining angry. I'm not saying this is easy," her voice broke. "Every day, sometime many times a day, I have to ask God to uproot the bitterness that tries to overwhelm me toward the people who did this to my baby. The Lord is teaching me through His Word that I can release all my anger and pain to him, and He will deal with those who have hurt us. God is teaching me how to take every thought captive and to stop the devil from tormenting me in my mind."

Pastor Wind squirmed uneasily in his seat. He felt conviction, but something else too. What was it…hope…was that it? Yes, a hope that maybe people could find answers even in hopeless situations. He looked over at Evelyn. Her eyes were shining with tears, but she was smiling. Judy, on his other side, continued to stare angrily at the floor.

212

Jenna handed the microphone back to her husband. "Well, I guess that's it."

"We're not public speakers," Raymond said, "but we wanted you all to know that things have changed for us. We feel like we're just beginning to learn what life is all about. I guess we never understood before that we're in a war and we are either on God's side or the Devil's. When we hang on to anger, bitterness, blame, or unforgiveness toward anyone, we are telling God that we can take care of things better than He can. We spent this last week with Philip and Phoebe, and they have been showing us in scripture how much God loves us. One other thing. I always thought God is going to do whatever he wants, so why pray? I thought God would have his way, after all, He's God. Tony showed me in the scriptures where it says that it's not God's will that any should perish. That got me thinking. People perish and go to Hell every day, but it's not God's will. God gave us all free will, and we can either receive what he has for us or not."

Taking a handkerchief out of his pocket, Ray dabbed at the tears streaming down his face. "I know this isn't over yet, we're still walking through the valley of the shadow of death. Sometimes the pain is unbearable, and I have so many questions, but we're finally getting to know the Good Shepherd. We are finally getting to know how good

213

God is, even when bad things happen." As he handed the microphone back to Philip, he put his arm around Jenna. Although she was now openly crying, there was a radiant glow on her face.

Philip looked across the little group and said, "I believe we have some people here tonight who are hurting. Maybe you've suffered the loss of someone you love and are angry at God. Maybe you have pain in your body. Let's all agree to partner with Jesus tonight. Jesus is our Healer and He said, 'Be it unto you according to your faith.' As far as I know, we are all believers here tonight. Even if you aren't, God wants you to know you can be. Just say yes to Jesus. Say yes to Him to be your Savior. Say yes to Him to be your Healer. He is just waiting for you to partner with Him, to agree with Him, so please just say yes."

Philip closed his eyes and led everyone in a simple prayer. As he opened his eyes to dismiss, he noticed the side door closing quietly, and three folding chairs in the back row were now empty.

Chapter Thirty-Six

There was no talking on the way home. Evelyn and Don Wind stared straight ahead. Judy, in the back seat, was also deep in thought, her mind racing. Don at last broke the silence.

"Do you girls want to stop for coffee?"

"I do," Judy answered. "This Bible study, or whatever they call it, has me so confused."

Don pulled into a familiar diner and after they were seated in a booth, Evelyn spoke first. "I believe we have misjudged these children and also Philip and Phoebe Brown. It seems they really are helping people."

Don was defensive. "I never said our church was the only one with the answers."

Evelyn, with a slight agitation in her voice, confronted him as only a wife can. "No, you have never said those exact words, but you have certainly acted like it."

Judy interrupted before he could answer. "Pastor, what has happened to these young people? Is this a good thing? I tried to find something wrong with what they were saying, but I felt like, well, like they really know God, know Him in a way that I never have. In fact, they make me feel like I don't know Him at all. That can't be right…can it?"

"The thing I noticed was how happy and energetic everyone was. They all looked so…well…so alive! Especially the Harrison's and Tony after all they've been through," Evelyn added.

Don Wind was once again remembering how it was in seminary. *I was that way once upon a time,* he thought. *What happened to me? When did the care of running the church start to choke out my joy and faith? When did preparing a sermon become just another task instead of a joyful expectation of presenting God's Word? Why did my church members have to go to a couple of retailers for the love of God?* Don was startled by what he was thinking! *Yes, it was the love of God! My people found the love of God at Philip and Phoebe's Bible study. That's why they were drawn there! I've let these people down. No, God, I've let you down. I've taught rules, but I've lost my first love. Doing anything just because it is a rule, whether it is God's rule or man's church rule, will never bring the kind of life I saw in those young people tonight. How could I have forgotten all of this?*

A perky waitress interrupted his thoughts.

Just coffee," he said, dismissing her.

"Decaf for all of us," Evelyn added, "and extra cream for me please."

Seeing the dejected look on Don's face, Evelyn softened. "I'm not blaming you, Don, it just seems like our church, actually our whole denomination, is all about rules. Why don't *we* teach people about a relationship with God? These people seem to have woven God into every area of their lives! I can't say I've done that. They pray about everything!"

Judy sat contemplating all that was being said, and then asked, "But Evelyn, isn't that a little fanatical? I mean, come on, we live in the real world. We're not in heaven yet. Is it possible to live that way?"

Don, drawn back into the conversation by Judy's intensive look, tried to think of something wise and profound to answer, but his mind felt like mush. He was beginning to see himself as a balloon with a slow leak, becoming smaller and smaller in his own eyes.

He finally answered, surprising himself by what came out of his mouth. "Judy, we've been friends for a lot of years. I think I can be candid with you. I…saw something tonight, and I'm not going to pretend I didn't. Somehow… somewhere, I have let my people down. Why would they go to a shop owner for the love of God if I am meeting their spiritual needs in church?" *There it is again, I can't get away from it, can I God? They went looking for your love. They went because they couldn't find faith in your love in my sermons...or in me.*

The two women watched as Pastor Wind played with his napkin, folding and refolding it, then twisting it like a rope and tying it in a knot. Evelyn placed her hand on his, stopping the nervous gesture. "It's okay," she said, patting his hand. "Maybe we just worship differently than this...these...other people. Do we even know where Philip and Phoebe go to church?"

"I'm not going to say it doesn't matter to me where they go to church. I do have some ideas about doctrine that will not be easily changed, but what I saw tonight doesn't have as much to do with doctrine as with obedience to God's Word. The first law of the Lord is love, and...well, do you ladies recall the Sunday school lesson I taught last week?"

"It was about the temple...the one Solomon built," Judy answered proudly. She was glad she remembered as her mind often wandered during his lessons.

"Yes, if you recall, I've been teaching from II Chronicles, where Solomon made an altar for sacrifices. Do you remember by any chance the description of that altar?"

Judy laughed nervously, "Well, let's see, I think I remember there was a big bronze altar, and didn't it have some kind of a tank or pool or something like that? Was it oxen or cows holding it up?"

"Yes, actually, the part you are talking about is exactly what I was thinking of. There was a large round tank made from bronze, and it was called *'The Sea'*. It was encircled just below its rim by two rows of figures that resembled oxen, and they were made from bronze."

Evelyn looked at him blankly. "Sooooo, what's your point?" she asked, slightly irritated. She hated it when he quizzed her about the minute points in his teaching.

"I was just thinking about another cow, that's all," he answered quietly. "That time it was a golden calf."

"You mean the story of the Israelites in the wilderness, right? They made a golden calf and worshiped it in defiance of God. But why are you talking about cows? I don't get it."

"What do you think Judy?"

"The golden calf was made in rebellion, but the bronze oxen were made out of obedience for worship," she chirped, as delighted as a school child who was the first with the answer.

"The people wanted to worship something they could see, so they made a golden calf, but God

219

directed Solomon to build the temple in a specific way, and part of that way was to make several bronze oxen," Don added.

"Okay, I see what you mean, that is, I think I do." Evelyn said, taking off her glasses and rubbing the creases on her forehead. "Are you trying to say that although it appears gold has more worth than bronze, if God directs you to build out of bronze, it better be bronze, not gold?"

Don chuckled at his wife's oversimplification of what appeared to him to be a spiritual revelation. "True, God blessed the bronze and cursed the gold in that case, but it's funny how a phrase keeps reverberating in your mind and…"

"But the people worshipped the calf, and those bronze things, well, they were just part of the temple. I mean, well, you know what I mean," Judy ended lamely.

"I guess I'm still not getting my point across. What I was trying to say, that is, what I think God is trying to show me, is that two things can look very similar and one can be wrong and the other can be right. Take our church and its traditions for instance. We have ways we have followed for decades. Sometimes I wonder if we have made the words of the men who founded our denomination more important to us than having a personal relationship with Jesus as our Lord. I've been so concerned with what the other leaders would think of me, that, well, I fear I've stopped being the person God called me to be. If I loved God the way I should, if I loved the people..."

Judy was confused by the troubled look in her pastor's eyes. She couldn't decide if she should be angry or contrite. *This church has been a landmark in our town for over one hundred years. My husband, my father, and my grandfather have all been elders in this church. Why does Tony have to rock the boat?* "I'm sorry, Pastor Wind. I should never have invited you to come with me tonight. I'm sorry Tony got messed up with these people."

"If I remember right, I invited myself, and please don't apologize. When I saw how these people prayed tonight, the sincerity and how they love God, how they worshiped Him with no thought of how others might perceive them, well, I guess I was a little jealous," he smiled sheepishly. "And another thing, something really strange happened to me tonight. As I said before, I kept thinking about bronze and gold and then, as I was sitting there listening, I started thumbing through my Bible. I bought my new one. I've been so excited about all of the footnotes."

"Don, will you please leave out all the details, and get to the point," Evelyn said, exasperated over yet another of Don's rabbit trails.

Don nodded and continued, "Well, as I was saying, my Bible fell open and I just started

221

reading. I guess I was trying to ignore what was going on around me." Don took the Bible out of his coat and turned some pages. Adjusting his glasses, he began to read, "Here in II Chronicles twelve, it says…"

"Please, Don, is this important?"

Don put the Bible back in his coat. "I guess I don't have to read it word for word. I just wanted to tell you that verse nine says that all of the shields that were made of gold were taken away from the king of Israel. Because they stopped trying to please God, they lost their gold to the king of Egypt."

"So?" Evelyn said. "What's your point?"

"I felt like God was trying to get my attention. They lost the gold, and then they replaced the gold shields they lost with bronze. The substitute that didn't have the value of the real was accepted with the same honor as the precious. Have I traded the relationship I once had with God for the doctrines of man? The men who founded our religion had a personal relationship with God. They learned the things that have been handed down to us because of that relationship. We mouth the things they learned and end up with bronze, not gold. I feel I've failed all of you. God wants you to have the gold."

"Bronze…gold…I'm sorry, Pastor Wind, but all of this sounds…well, no disrespect, but sometimes I have a hard time following all of your analogies. You have been a wonderful pastor! All these years you have been there for us."

"Have I? Have I, Judy? When Stanley died, when your daughter-in-law was killed, I didn't have any answers. To tell you the truth, I barely prayed for you because I just thought God was going to do whatever he wanted anyway, so why pray? What about the children that have been kidnapped and killed? I look in the paper and say, 'Oh isn't that terrible.' Tonight, as I listened to the Harris', I wondered, 'If I had taught our people the importance of praying, would this evil have taken our town?'"

"Is it too late?" Evelyn asked, her voice barely above a whisper.

"Too late for Brenda, yes, but not too late for me to change. I guess the first thing I need to do is repent, and then possibly…we could start a prayer group."

"I will come," Judy volunteered. "I'm not sure I understand all you're saying, but I want to."

"And you know I am always behind you, Dear."

As the three stood, Don Wind felt he was going in the right direction for the first time in a long while.

Evelyn slid out of the booth, and then she hesitated. "Wait a minute."

"What is it?"

"I...I...I don't have any pain!"

"What?"

"My back...when Philip asked us to agree with Jesus, I agreed!"

"You...what?"

"I just agreed, I said Jesus if you really can heal me, then I will agree with you to heal me, and....and I don't have any pain!"

"Can it be that simple?" Judy asked, amazed.

"I...I guess so," she said laughing. "Somehow when he said I could be healed if I believed, I thought to myself...I can believe. Philip said God would meet us at our ability to believe, through doctors or surgery or instantaneous miracles. He said we just need to believe God wanted us pain-free. That made sense to me, so I said, I believe!"

Don Wind paid the bill without commenting, choosing to ignore the stares of those in the restaurant who were trying to eavesdrop on his wife's exuberant demonstration of her new ability to bend and stretch. Deep inside he knew tonight had been a life-changing experience, and he wondered if it was too late to call Tony.

Chapter Thirty-Seven

"I wonder why they call it stir-crazy," Abby said aloud. She found she was talking to herself more and more. Well, at least I'm not answering myself, not usually anyway. They should call it a lack of stir…crazy. How can I keep from going crazy when there is no one to talk to?

The familiar click of the door and her captors once again made an entrance. They said few words, but she sensed compassion, especially in the old woman. The man seemed almost bored in his task and barely acknowledged her.

Abby talked continually from the time they entered until they left. Somehow, in the last few hours, she had moved from fear and panic into peace. The couple, although odd, seemed to be very anxious to make sure her needs were met and to please her in the best way possible.

As far as Abby could determine, she had been locked up for nearly a week. Time was hard to measure, but it seemed they came once a day. She began to count her days in solitary confinement by the count of her meals. She wanted a clock but decided she wouldn't press her luck.

After the first few days had passed, Abby asked for a writing tablet. The old woman obliged and brought her a lined tablet, several pens, and some magazines. Hidden at the bottom of the stack of magazines was a Bible. *A strange thing for evil people to be smuggling in,* Abby thought. Opening the Bible almost superstitiously, she half expected it to be a ruse, but it truly was a Bible. Now she really was confused. If these people worked for Mrs. Musgrave and the others she'd heard talking on that fateful night, why were they keeping her alive? By the third day, Abby began to believe that perhaps her captors had rescued her. Gathering her courage, she finally asked why she was being held.

"Why, you're being protected, Child. Didn't Larry explain it to you?"

"But from whom and by whom?" Abby asked. "No one has explained anything to me."

"Oh, my darlin' girl. I'm so sorry, but I don't know anything," the old woman explained. "I only know it involves some very evil people and it's very dangerous for anyone to see that you're still alive. I know this isn't the best of accommodations, but we can't risk movin' you and them finding out you're still alive. Just sit tigh,t and I promise you this will all be over soon."

Those few words gave her comfort and a measure of hope and she stopped wailing.

In the beginning, she flipped through the magazines, paced, and tried to find a way to get to the grate in the ceiling. Although the old woman had warned her to sit tight, she continued to make plans to escape. Her captors had not brought another chair, and Abby decided they were onto her. Bored with the magazines, she tried sketching and journaling. Restless, she spent a lot of time reading the Bible and trying to understand what she read.

Each time her captors came, the man stood in front of the door while the old woman set the tray beside the bed, cleaned up, and straightened whatever needed to be taken care of.

Sitting on the bed with her knees drawn up under her chin, Abby watched them cautiously. The woman's eyes seemed to shine with delight when she noticed the Bible opened beside the kerosene lamp. Hopeful for a response, Abby once more tried to engage the woman in conversation. "Thank you for the Bible. You must be a Christian."

"Baptized since nearly forty years back," the woman smiled.

Tonight, as well as the usual meal, the woman carried a large bottle. "Kerosene," was all she said. She turned quickly and was gone before Abby could question her more.

The metal door clanged shut, and Abby looked at the meal, pot roast with carrots and potatoes. Her eyes filled with tears as she thought of her mother fixing this meal and scolding her for not having an appetite.

"Oh Mom," she cried, "will I ever see you again?"

Heartsick, Abby knelt beside the bed. The cement was cold on her knees, the wool blanket rough to her face. Her tears ran unchecked as she prayed.

"Dear God, I don't know quite how to say this, but here goes. I've been reading your book and from what I read, I kind of think I need to ask you to forgive me for not believing in You or your Son. I'm sorry, God. I do believe in you now and I believe in your Son, Jesus. It's not just because I'm locked up either. I guess I see what Ellen was talking about. I do want your help. God, I don't know what's going to happen to me. But God, if I die, I want to be with you. If I ever get out of here," her face contorted and her voice broke with a sob. "When I get out of here, I'm going to tell everyone how you saved my life." She stood up and looked at the food. "Oh, and P.S. God," she said looking toward the ceiling, "thanks for the food, but I sure could use a bath and a change of clothes. I don't know how you can accomplish this, but while you're at it, I'd like a head wash." She laughed and dove into the potatoes.

Chapter Thirty-Eight

Discouragement came in waves, and then, the next day, the two came into the room with a five-gallon bucket of warm water, a towel, a washcloth, shampoo, and a complete change of clothes. The tags were still on the clothing, and Abby surmised that the old woman had bought them herself. *I can't believe that crooked cop cares what happens to me, so I wonder if somehow these people have rescued me from him.* She gasped, *I wonder if they killed him? Maybe these people are crazy and are just waiting for the right time to kill me too. Maybe they brought the Bible because they didn't want me to go to hell when they...* The thought was too terrible to comprehend, but Abby had read about cults that did horrid things in the name of religion.

Besides the clothing, towels, and other personal items, they finally brought her a chair, a sturdy straight-backed chair. She tried not to show her exuberance at the possibility of escape. It seemed that the old woman took an unusually slow time in loading her discarded dishes into a box and exchanging her chamber pot for a clean one. *If I weren't so terrified, this would be humiliating,* she thought.

At last, Abby heard the familiar click as the key turned in the lock at their departure. *I'd better wait awhile, this could be a trick.* She tiptoed over to the door and listened. *What good does this do? That door must be six inches thick.*

Relying on the pattern of her captors coming only once a day, she stripped off her grimy clothes and bathed as well as one can in a two-gallon pail of water. First of all, she washed and towel-dried her hair, bemoaning the fact that her hair was so long. Then she sponged as well as she could saying, "Oh, thank you, God, for warm water." Slipping on the clean underclothes, sweatpants, and socks, she continued to whisper praises to God. She wadded up her dirty clothes and set them with the bucket by the door.

Without a watch, it was hard to determine the time. They usually brought her a hot meal along with a sandwich and fruit wrapped in waxed paper. Supposing the hot meal was brought at six o'clock, Abby determined to wait at least six hours before trying to escape. *What if they brought my hot meal at noon and left the sandwich and fruit for supper? In that case, it would probably be better to wait twelve hours.* She finally decided twelve hours would be safer as she couldn't imagine that they would bring her roast beef and potatoes for breakfast.

Having no idea of her whereabouts, she determined wherever she was, it would be safer to try to escape under the cover of darkness. Deciding to try and count the twelve hours, she lamented briefly that she had forgotten to put her watch on the fateful day of her capture.

After slowly counting to sixty she would put one finger in the air. When all ten fingers were counted, she made an X on the paper. When she had six Xs in a row, she made an H to stand for one hour. Because her mind wandered and she sometimes lost count, she decided she must be close to twelve hours when she was actually closer to eleven.

Once again, Abby pulled the table onto the bed, then the chair onto the table, and finally the magazines on top of the chair. Standing on tiptoe, she could now reach the vent. "Okay, okay, calm down, Abby, you can do this," she reassured herself. She had stuffed one of her shoes under her shirt so she could use it to pound on the rusty nails and still have both hands free until she got her balance. *Up and up, so far so good. Now, if I can just get my fingers in the grate...YES!*

Holding the grate with one hand, she pounded the rusty screws with her shoe. Just as she thought, the screws began to crumble. Flecks of rust and dust flew onto her head and face as she hit the grate over and over.

Hallelujah, it's loose! Abby gave the grate a huge pull and it came loose. She threw it aside. Gripping the two-by-four that framed the edge of the opening, she was able to pull herself through. Her legs and feet dangled, kicking the air, as she pulled her torso up into a large room above. Swinging one leg up and pushing off, she managed to be free of the cell below.

Panting, she looked around. There was a layer of dust coating everything. *So much for feeling clean,* she thought. In the jubilation of possible freedom, her heart was racing.

She stood and surveyed the room. It was made of concrete blocks, but there was a small window on the far side. The window was too high for her to see out, but a soft light seeped through the dirty cobweb-covered pane. Daylight? *Forget leaving under the cover of darkness. Can it be morning?*

As her eyes grew accustomed to the dim light, she noticed a stairway going down on one side of the room. *That must go to my cell,* she shuddered, peeking down the stairwell at the large metal door. On the other side of the room was a stairway going up.

Tiptoeing up the stairs, she came to a slanted door. She pushed as hard as she could, but it wouldn't budge. The adrenaline rush of escape had energized her, but now she felt like giving up. *God, where are you?* Sitting on the top stair leading to the slanted cellar door, she looked down and noticed two wooden doors. *More rooms. Oh please, God, let one lead to an escape.*

The first room proved to be a wine cellar, empty of bottles with only rack after rack where wine was once stored. There was a small window, but, even from the floor, it looked as if it was painted shut. She tried the other door. It opened stiffly, dragging over the rough cement floor. This room was empty as well, but just enough light came through the small window in the main room to outline a coal chute coming from the top of the wall near the ceiling. The problem was the metal chute stopped about four feet from the ground, and Abby wasn't sure it would hold her weight. *Please, God, help me! What should I do?*

Going back to the wine racks, she tried moving them, to no avail. As her eyes grew more accustomed to the dim light, she noticed a large wooden keg at the back of the room. It was empty but still quite heavy. Pushing with all of her might, she was able to push the keg over and then roll it to the door. Once through the door, she rolled the keg on its side across the main room. Tipping it back to an upright position, she shoved it and was able to move it under the coal chute.

Okay, God, I believe you are helping me.
Onto the barrel she climbed. Grasping the metal coal chute with both hands, she laboriously and slowly climbed the rusty, wobbly slide. It creaked loudly with every movement, and she was terrified her captors would come to see what all the noise was about. As she pulled her body towards the small tin door, she prayed she would be able to squeeze through the tiny door once she reached the top. Pushing herself through the door, she squinted at the sky and realized the small amount of light coming through the cellar's windows was the light of streetlights and it was sometime in the night. Horrified, she also now realized she had been in the cellar of the bridal shop all along.

Now she stood on the lawn and looked up at the house where she had heard the voices. Terrified, she had no idea of how to contact anyone or where to go for help. "What next God? Where can I go?"

Chapter Thirty-Nine

Joan slipped off the examining table and began to dress. She was shaking with resentment and fear and her eyes began to well up with tears as she reflected on the doctor's test results. "You're in fine physical shape, Mrs. Ellington. You haven't been married long. I'm sure you'll conceive soon. Just give God and nature a chance. You and your husband are certainly anxious to begin your family," he joked lightly.

God and nature have nothing to do with this. I can't believe I went to the humiliation of throwing myself at that bartender and still I've not conceived. All the trouble I went to, all the lies. Well, Peter may have powers, but obviously he can't read my mind the way Katrina can. If he did, he wouldn't have believed me when I told him I wanted some time to myself to shop on the island and surprise him with a special gift. He was so disappointed when I told him I couldn't find anything that was unique or special enough.

"Here's the prescription to stop the vomiting," the nurse said, smiling gently.

Okay, so the doctor said the vomiting was caused by my nerves. I can't believe he said it was psychosomatic, like I'm a crazy person. He probably wonders why someone married to Peter would have anything to be stressed about.

"Under stress," she whispered as she turned the key and started her new Corvette. She cursed as familiar nausea threatened again. *Why would I be under stress? I just caught the most eligible bachelor in the county, maybe in the state! I've just returned from a honeymoon that anyone in their right mind would die for. Of course, there was no lovemaking, and I had to play the harlot with someone who might have given me a social disease. Why didn't I get pregnant? It was the right time of the month. I counted the days. Katrina probably put a hex on anyone who would touch me. Under stress! Why wouldn't I be under stress, unless you consider that I've just married a lunatic...unless you considered that now I will have to commit a murder...not the murder of someone who deserves to die, but an innocent child!* Joan screamed in anguish, pounding the steering wheel.

She knew she was driving too fast, but she didn't care. She almost hoped the police would stop her, lock her up, and throw away the key. *No, that's not true. I don't want to go to jail. I don't want to be*

237

convicted of murder either. I just want to get out of this trap.

"Oh God, help me!" She could not believe she had called on God. *Why would God help me now? He has never helped me before. He never once stopped my father when he beat me within an inch of my life. He never once stopped the mouth of my stepmother and her vile insinuations.*

Unbidden, the picture of Jill and Jennifer came into her mind, and she groaned in despair. Lois was always babysitting those two, parading them under her nose, telling her the cute things they'd said or done. *Why does it have to be someone I know? The town is full of kids.* She could hear Peter's voice, soft and hypnotic.

"It's more of a sacrifice if you know the child, Joan." That soft gentle voice she had once loved had turned to abhorrence. The seduction, the irresistible pleasure she had felt at his lightest touch, had turned to repulsion.

I've got to get away. If I try, will Peter kill me? The answer rang in her mind. *Yes,* she was sure of it. *It will be just like Thorton, but if I go to the police, who will believe me?*

Peter said the police were on his side. If I drive to another county, another town, or another state, will they be able to find me? I have my bank account. I could draw all the money out. That's

238

what I'll do! I'll get a divorce and change my name. I have skills. I can start over far from here.

Thoughts of escape were temporarily aborted when she pulled into her driveway. *My beautiful home, everything I've ever dreamed of. How can I leave all of this? I can't go...I can't stay!* Sighing deeply, she rested her head on the steering wheel.

They said I didn't have to be involved. I wasn't there before. I don't know anything for sure. If I went to the police, would I be arrested as an accomplice? If I just came clean and said I had no idea they were trafficking children and drugs and that I knew nothing about the death of the Harrison child, would they believe me? Will they think I'm crazy? What if I tell the police that I just found out what these maniacs were up to. Would the police believe me? Maybe I should just run away, file for divorce, and sue Peter for everything he's worth. But what about Katrina? She will never let me escape.

Joan threw the car into reverse and made up her mind. *I'll withdraw as much money as possible and drive to another state. Maybe a state halfway across the country. I'll turn myself in. I'm a pretty good actress, I'll just make the police believe I'm innocent.*

She pressed her foot down on the accelerator. *The sooner I get out of this state, the better. I know*

I'm not a good person, but I'm not like these devil worshipers. I'm not a murderer, I'm not...

Fumbling for a cigarette, her purse fell onto the floor. Groping clumsily, she swore and reached down, trying to retrieve her purse.

Her eyes had left the road for only a second. Looking up, she realized she was almost in the ditch. Yanking the steering wheel, she overcompensated, causing the car to swerve wildly. The last thing Joan Ellington saw was a man looking down at her from the cab of a semi, his mouth open in a silent scream as he laid on the horn.

Chapter Forty

Peter paced, checking his watch every ten minutes. Katrina Polworth would be waiting anxiously by the phone. He had promised to call as soon as Joan returned from the doctor's office. Luciferians around the world were anxiously anticipating the conception of their long-awaited *Messiah*.

As the afternoon wore on, with no word from Joan, he began to worry. *Perhaps she's shopping*, he thought, *but surely not. She must realize how excited everyone is to hear the good news. Katrina is beside herself with joy and anticipation. This is the child we've been waiting for. We should be celebrating by now. Joan shouldn't make Katrina wait. She won't like it.*

At three o'clock the phone rang at the Ellington residence. Peter picked it up hollering "Joan where are you?" There were a few seconds of silence on the other end. Then a female voice spoke, "Mr. Ellington?"

"Yes, I'm sorry, I was expecting my wife."

"I'm sorry to have to tell you this but, Mr. Ellington, there's been an accident. This is Livingston Hospital calling…Mr. Ellington?"

"Yes?"

"Your wife has been in an automobile accident."

"And…"

"I'm sorry, Sir, it's…pretty bad."

"I'll be right there."

Pushing down the button, he quickly dialed Katrina. She listened silently. When she finally spoke, her voice was flat and void of emotion. "I knew it."

"What?"

"The little witch has betrayed us."

"What are you talking about?"

"I've been sitting here waiting for the confirmation. As I sat meditating this afternoon, the spirits told me she had betrayed us. Because she refused to cooperate, she had to be stopped, so they stopped her."

"The woman calling from the hospital said she's still alive. Will she die?"

"Of course she'll die, you stupid idiot!"

He didn't know what to say and stood silently trembling.

"She could have had everything, everything!" she hissed. "Now we'll have to find a new candidate, a woman who realizes the honor of bringing forth the promised one." She swore again and then asked, "How much does she know?"

"Well…I inferred…I was careful to never tell her the details."

"What do you mean, you inferred?"

"I told her a virgin, a young child, would have to be sacrificed if she didn't conceive."

"You told her what?"

"Katrina, you told me she would have to choose a child. The letters have been sent. I…I was preparing her," he whined. "She knew about the Harrison child and the others. I thought you would be pleased."

"You fool! I never told you to tell her about the Harrison child!" She was screaming curses at him with every other word. "I'll meet you at the hospital. More than likely, she's not had an opportunity to betray us, and she won't…do you understand?"

"Yes, of course," he answered contritely.

Placing the phone back on its cradle, he took out a handkerchief and mopped the sweat from his brow.

What now, what now? Pacing back and forth, he ran his hand repeatedly through his hair. Glancing in the mirror over the mantel, he stared hopelessly at his ashen reflection. *I have tried so hard to do everything right. What is money without power? Will Katrina choose someone else to play the part of the savior's father? I must prove to her that I can be trusted. I hate you for this, Joan! You deserve to die. How could you betray me like this?* He now detested Joan with the same intensity he had previously desired her. If she was not already dead, she soon would be. He would make sure of it.

~~~

Mary Catherine stood at the hospital pay phone making call after call. The coins went into the slot, clanging their metal tones.

"Phoebe? Thank God, I've finally reached someone. I decided to go home for lunch today. A mile from home, I came around the corner, and there were police cars everywhere…and two ambulances. Phoebe, it's Joan, Joan Ellington."

Lowering her voice, she whispered, "It doesn't look good. Her car was hit by a semi. I think the truck driver is okay from what I overheard, but Joan is in pretty bad shape. Someone said she went through the windshield. I've called Lois, but I've not been able to reach anyone else. No, I'm fine, Phoebe…no really. I'm just so concerned about Joan. I don't know her very well, but…well…I'm pretty sure she isn't a believer. Wait a minute. I think the doctors just left her room. I'll try to find out what I can, but I don't know if they'll let me in. You'll come down? Oh, thank goodness. Can you try and get a hold of the Bible study people to pray? Good, good…yes. Will you call Ellen? I've run out of change. Tell her she's in room two twenty. I'll see you in a few minutes then…yes…yes…thank you."

Looking through the window of the intensive care room, Mary caught her breath. Joan was a tangle of tubes and cords. A nurse came up behind her as she started to enter. "I'm sorry, ma'am, you can't go in unless you're a relative. Are you a relative?"

Mary Catherine dropped her eyes, "Ah, no…just a concerned friend."

"Well, I"m sorry, you can't go in."

Mary backed away as Peter and an older woman stepped off the elevator. Rushing past Mary, he stopped at the nurse's station.

"I'm Peter Ellington. Where's my wife?"

"This way, Mr. Ellington. She hasn't regained consciousness, but we have managed to stop the bleeding." Mary was right on his heels trying to hear what was being said. The nurse turned just before opening the door for Peter, "The doctor will be free to talk to you in just a moment. Please stop by the desk…and you are?" she asked Katrina.

"Her mother."

"Yes, you can come in, but only for a few minutes."

Mary Catherine watched in amazement. She knew very little about Joan, but she knew Joan's mother died years ago.

The nurse stayed in the room as Peter and Katrina stared at the pale, bruised, and bandaged figure. After a moment, the nurse motioned for the two to leave. They followed her out of the room reluctantly, whispering as they headed for the nurse's station.

Chapter Forty-One

"Those people," Katrina spit out the words, motioning with her head toward the tiny group standing in the hall. "Who are they and what are they doing here?"

Overhearing Katrina's remark, Lois tried to help.

"The girl with the black hair is Ellen Evans. She lives at our house. Mary Catherine Larson is the pregnant one. She works with me. The guy is Tony Sands. He lives across the street from us. I think I heard Mary call the woman with gray hair Phoebe. Let me think…if I remember right…her name is Phoebe Brown. I babysit for Tony and Mary Catherine when they go to the Brown's Bible study."

Having stopped crying long enough to identify everyone, Lois blew her nose noisily and asked Peter if he knew anything yet. He shook his head and stared at the floor.

Katrina zeroed in on Lois when she heard Phoebe's name. "Did you say Phoebe Brown?" she asked, glaring at the group.

"I'm not sure. I'll go ask her if you like. Do you know if she is a friend of Joan's?" Lois asked innocently.

"Get them out of here, do you hear me?" Katrina hissed. "I know for a fact that Joan wants nothing to do with those people. Peter, do something!"

Peter stood looking as if he didn't know what to do or how to approach them. Lois volunteered, "I'll talk to them."

Tiptoeing up to the group, she whispered, "Katrina and Peter are upset by your presence."

"You bet they are," Phoebe said a little too loudly.

Tony put his finger to his lips. "Shush-h-h," he whispered, "let's go to the hospital chapel and pray."

Lois looked nervously over her shoulder at Peter and Katrina. "I think they meant for you to leave the hospital. Katrina says you're bringing bad karma."

Mary patted Lois's arm, "It's okay, Lois, it doesn't matter what they think. All that matters is Joan."

Lois walked back to Peter as the little group of prayers started toward the elevator.

"I want them out of the building! Did you tell them Peter wants them out of the building?"

"I tried," Lois said meekly.

Katrina looked at her with venom, and Lois stepped back, fearing she would strike her.

"I'm calling the others together," Katrina said. "Make sure you do what needs to be done."

Peter nodded in compliance.

"Why don't you go too, Lois," Peter said. "They won't let you in to see her, and there's nothing you can do to help."

Lois, feeling like a naughty child who was sent to her room, started toward the elevator. Entering, she pushed the button. The doors opened, and she exited but was halfway down the hall before she realized she was on the wrong floor. Hurrying back to the elevator, she pushed the down button and waited. The elevator did not come. She pushed it again…nothing.

Out of the corner of her eye, she saw a sign, 'CHAPEL', with an arrow pointing to her left. Hesitating, she took a deep breath. *I don't want to be alone,* she thought. *Tony said they were going to the chapel to pray. I wish I knew if you're real God.*

Walking slowly toward the chapel door, she pushed it open as quietly as possible and sat in the back. Ellen, Mary, and Phoebe were kneeling at an altar praying silently. Tony sat in the front row, his

249

head bowed, his hands folded. She listened as he petitioned for Joan's life to be spared.

Desiring with all her heart to be one of those calling on the Almighty for mercy, she choked out a sob, betraying her presence.

Mary Catherine turned and opened her eyes. Tiptoeing to the back of the room, she sat beside Lois and placed her hand gently on her trembling back. Lois covered her face with both hands and started to sob. Mary slipped her arm around her and handed her a tissue. After a few moments, Lois stood as if to leave. The others stood too.

"I don't know why this is hitting me so hard. We really aren't that close. I shouldn't be here. I don't…I don't…" her voice broke, and she began to cry again.

"Belong?" Phoebe asked softly.

Lois nodded.

"Jesus wants all of us to belong to Him."

"What?" Lois questioned.

"Yes," Phoebe smiled. "It's really quite simple."

"Just ask Him to come and live in your heart," Mary said. "You do want Him to, don't you?"

Lois nodded. "I want to believe, but I don't know how to pray. I want to know God the way…the way you do, Ellen. You talk about Him as if He's real. As if He's right beside you, as if He wants to help you! When I hear all of you talking, I

250

always think it would be the most wonderful thing in the world to be able to believe the way you do, to believe you can make a difference, to believe God loves you and has a plan for your life."

"You can," Tony whispered. "You can believe, Lois."

"It's not that easy for me. You don't understand. You see…there…are things…things you don't know about me. I've done terrible things. I've got to get my life straightened out first and…"

Tony placed his hands gently on either side of Lois' face, "Lois, God's Word says that all have sinned and fall short of the glory of God. In God's eyes, all sin separates us from Him. Your sins and my sins are the same in the sight of God."

"But how…I mean…how can I have a…relationship with God? I guess I don't understand."

"When we ask Jesus to forgive us of our sins and to come and live inside of us, He does."

"But…how can He live inside of everyone at the same time? I don't think I understand."

"Well, that's where the Holy Spirit comes in. To tell you the truth, I can't explain it very well, but Phoebe can…Phoebe?"

"Let's sit down," Phoebe said. Taking Lois's hand in hers, she started to explain. "Lois, receiving Jesus is a step of faith. Jesus said if you believe with your heart and confess with your lips that

Jesus is Lord…well, He comes into your spirit and makes you a brand-new person."

Lois turned to Mary, "Like you tried to tell me in the office that day? Like when it happened to you?"

"Yes," Mary nodded.

"I thought it would be hard, I thought I had to be good enough first."

The other four laughed softly. "We all thought that at first," Ellen said. "That's one of Satan's lies. That's how he keeps people from believing. You see, none of us can ever be good enough. That's why we need Jesus."

"Okay, what do I say?"

"Just say, Jesus, I believe in you. I want you to live inside of me and take control of my life. I want you to take my sin away and make me brand new."

Lois repeated the simple prayer. She was quiet for a moment, but when she lifted her head and looked at them, her face was filled with wonder.

"That's it?" she asked. "That's all there is to it? I can't believe that all these years I've made it so hard! I don't understand it, but I know something happened to me."

The others laughed and took turns hugging her.

Lois asked Phoebe if she had any more tissues. Laughing, she held up a tattered piece of Kleenex. "I think I've been a bit like this Kleenex," Lois laughed. "But now I really have hope. And you know what else?"

Her new friends waited expectantly.

"I believe God heard your prayers and somehow I believe Joan is going to make it."

Chapter Forty-Two

Sergeant Larry Grant handed his keys to the valet, slipped from behind the wheel of his squad car, and followed Detective Carson Layman into the restaurant.

"Nice place," Layman remarked.

"Yes, it's new. It's only been open a year."

"Can you afford this on a policeman's salary?" Layman joked.

"Not really, but it's pretty quiet in here this time of day, and even though I doubt anyone in this town would know who you are, I wanted to talk where we'd have complete privacy. This is definitely not one of the local hangouts."

The maître d' showed them to a table in the corner, and Larry ordered appetizers.

"So, you've found the first two missing children. Have you notified their parents?" Larry asked.

"Yes, we have both little girls in protective custody. Finding two-year-old Mary Jane Johnston was the beginning. She was sold to a couple who were unable to pass the standard adoption qualifications. We found her in Jonesboro Mississippi. I believe the adoptive parents paid a pretty penny for that little girl and are heartsick about giving her up, but they're cooperating."

"How in the world did you find them?"

"It was a fluke. The child started running a temperature and they took her to the emergency room. One of our guys just happened to be in there getting patched up from a car wreck. He heard the interns talking about the pentagram scar on her torso."

"And you think that was a fluke?" Larry asked, smiling broadly. "I'd call that divine intervention, but I wonder why the couple that had her didn't notify the police."

"Well, it's pretty evident they knew her adoption was arranged under shady circumstances. I'm sure they didn't want to do anything to cause the authorities to ask questions. Although they were too old to go through proper channels, I believe they are good people, and when it came to the child's health, they weren't willing for her to come to harm."

"And the second child, where did you find her?"

"She ended up in Indianapolis. I guess she's got quite a vocabulary for a three-year-old. A daycare worker notified the police when the child kept telling stories about having a new mommy and daddy. She said she had to move because somebody made a mark on her tummy. The caregiver ignored the story at first, but one day the child asked her if she wanted to see the mark and lifted her shirt."

"Wow, I imagine the worker was pretty upset when she saw the pentagram scar."

"Yes, she called the police right away, but first she called the woman who had enrolled the child in the daycare. By the time the authorities checked the couple's apartment, they were gone, but we have the child, and we've notified her parents."

"You aren't afraid this will get back to Katrina?"

"I think Katrina was smart enough to keep her name out of it. I doubt if anyone could trace it back to her even if they wanted to. We're trying to keep it quiet for now. I know the children's parents are suffering, but hopefully, we'll have this thing wrapped up in the next few days, and we'll be able to return the children into the arms of their waiting parents. I'm sure just knowing their children are alive and are in safekeeping…"

"Of course, they're relieved," Larry interrupted. "If only Richard Thorton had talked."

"And the accident was no accident?"

"Well, he had been drinking, but the breaks were cut."

"And so, we have another murder we can chock up to Polworth and her little group of followers, but you never got anything out of him?"

"No, he died instantly in the crash. I just wish I could have convinced him to point the finger at Katrina."

"It's obvious they couldn't let him live. His drinking made him too much of a liability. Have you been able to get anything out of any of the others in the group?"

"We've been focused on the daycare since all three girls were enrolled there," Larry said, picking up the menu. "But until last week, there was nothing to tie the abductions to the Luciferians."

A waiter came and they ordered.

Detective Carson waited until the waiter was out of earshot before asking, "What do you know about the owners of the daycare?"

"It's owned by Ellington Industries. During the war, a lot of women had to work, and babysitters were hard to find. I'm sure the senior Ellington is innocent, but the younger Ellington, Peter, has been involved with Katrina for a long time. All the workers are very concerned and affirm their innocence, but I won't be surprised to find some of them belong to the cult. They all seem to be upstanding citizens on the surface, and yet…"

"Now I can see why your mayor brought me in on this. I guess he didn't trust anyone here in Cloverton."

"Yes, it's not that we suspected anyone on the force, but there would always be someone who shared with their brother, wife, or best friend. We couldn't take the chance that it might get back to Katrina."

"When did Mayor Hamilton have you join the Luciferians?"

"It wasn't exactly his idea, and to tell you the truth, they never trusted me enough to let me in on their meetings. At first, I thought they were just trafficking drugs, but shortly after I looked the other way, the little girls started disappearing. For a while, we reasoned we were dealing with a serial killer. The problem was, we never found any bodies. It never occurred to us Polworth was involved in both crimes."

"You knew they were dealing in drugs."

"Yes, I was trying to get enough evidence to get the top person and stop the drug trafficking, but this child abduction was a whole new ballgame."

"And when did you begin to suspect Katrina?"

"Well, I know this probably sounds crazy, but my mother has a little prayer group. Every time they prayed about the missing girls, the name Katrina Polworth would pop into my mom's head.

Finally, she wrote the name down and asked her ladies if anyone knew her. They didn't, but when I came home that night, she asked me, and I about fell over. Our police department has used Katrina's psychic abilities for years. I was against it, but who am I? I didn't tell anyone on the force. I just went to Mayor Hamilton. He and I have known each other since I was a kid, and I knew I could trust him. He encouraged me to try and get close to Polworth. It wasn't easy, but the fact the department used her in the past gave me a leg up."

"I'm surprised you didn't think your mom was getting that name so you'd go to Katrina for help."

"Are you kidding? The way my mom explains things, this psychic stuff is just an imitation of what God wants to do. You would be amazed at the answers these women get when they pray. Although my mom knew that Polworth and her group were on the side of evil, her prayer group continued to pray that somehow these…these devil worshipers would see the truth and give their lives to Jesus."

Detective Layman shook his head slowly. "Incredible, I'm half tempted to believe," he chuckled. "But to tell you the truth, I usually just put these things in the same basket of eggs, you know, aliens, angels, demons, God. If I can't explain it, I leave it alone."

Setting the food in front of the two gentlemen, the waiter asked if there would be anything else. Larry smiled and dismissed him. He could tell Carson Layman was having a hard time with the conversation and was thankful for the interruption.

Larry continued, "At first, I was a little nervous…I mean, I was afraid you Feds would come in and mess things up. Now I realize we needed your help."

"Well, once they took a child across the state line, it became a federal case. I have several people working undercover, but we still can't figure out how the abductions are made. It's almost as if they just disappear out of their beds…no sign of forced entry or struggle. I'm sure you've considered the parents could be part of the cult. Is there any possibility they're just handing their children over to Katrina? Maybe the parents are Luciferians too."

"I wondered about that at first, but as I got to know each family… well…I just don't believe it. If only Thorton had lived. That night when I took him home because he was too drunk to drive, he kept mumbling something about the little girl's death. He would cry and say it was all an accident."

"You think they didn't mean to kill the Harrison girl?"

"I don't know. I know they took the children for their secret ceremonies. That's evident from the pentagram carved on their torso. I don't even want to imagine what else they've done. There are cases in New York City where women got pregnant so they could sacrifice their newborn babies. I guess this cult goes back thousands of years before Jesus. They were very big in France right after the turn of the century, and some of them migrated to America."

"It's pretty amazing the way they stay underground."

Larry waved to the waiter for the check. "I guess that's about all for now. If you come up with anything new, you have my private number."

"Yes, it shouldn't be long."

The valet brought the car. They got in, and Larry adjusted his rearview mirror. Carson was talking about catching a plane, but Larry was only half listening. Something was nagging him. *What is it, God? I feel like I'm so close to the answer and yet...*

Larry watched as a nicely dressed older couple got out of their car. They handed their keys to the valet. "I've got it!"

"What?"

"Forget about catching that plane," Larry said.

Detective Layman looked puzzled as Larry raced out of the parking lot, his siren blaring.

Chapter Forty-Three

Peter sat beside the lump of bandages, tubes, and wires that had once been his beautiful wife. Katrina had given the order, and he knew she was right. *All I have to do is pinch her nostrils. No one will even question it. No one expects her to live anyway. I can cover her mouth with one hand and pinch her nostrils with the other. She is unconscious. She won't even struggle. There won't be an autopsy, she's barely alive.*

Peter felt the perspiration dripping down the back of his neck. He had never hurt anyone before. Even when he took the children, he was gentle with them. He was always careful to cover their nose with a chloroform-soaked cloth so they would go to sleep and not remember what happened to them.

I never meant to kill Brenda; she was such a beautiful child. I wanted her to be set aside for the glory of Lucifer. This is just a little setback. It's not my fault. I didn't choose Joan, Katrina did.

Peter sat beside the bed recalling the first time he had visited Katrina. In the beginning, it was just out of curiosity. When she told him he had been singled out for greatness, when she said he would become one of the most powerful men in the world, he surrendered to Lucifer, and that was when his whole life changed.

Why is everything askew? In his mind's eye, he saw the small group gathered in the hallway. *Joan should already be dead. Is there any way the prayers of those few are keeping her alive? That pregnant one was the first one on the scene. What kind of power does she have? Is she standing in the way of my future? She's already received an invitation to the restaurant. The stars are with me. I didn't even know what an enemy she was to the association when I sent the letters. The spirits are leading me. They won't let me down. The Sands' child is also on the list. Perhaps I should take both of them.* He laughed at the thought of it, remembering Tony from high school. *He was the star basketball player and president of the senior class. I hated him even then. Taking his daughter will be a real pleasure. Katrina will surely see I can be trusted if I show up with both of them. She told me I have the power to be invisible, and it must be true! How else have I been able to take the children without being seen or even detected?*

The very thought of it and his adrenalin started pumping. He put his head back, closed his eyes, and imagined the pain he could cause the parents. The power he felt was exhilarating. *It was so easy...so easy. I wonder if the keys have been made to Tony's house. I'll take care of Joan, and then I'll go to the restaurant.*

"Sorry, Joan," he whispered to the unconscious form. "We could have been so happy. You were so beautiful, but now I'm doing you a favor. Even if you live, you'll be scarred. You won't be happy living without your beauty." Peter slowly, deliberately placed one hand on Joan's mouth. "Goodbye, my dear", he whispered.

"Mr. Ellington?"

He jumped back, visibly shaken. "Yes?" he responded innocently.

"Mr. Ellington, I'm Detective Layman. I hate to bother you at a time like this, but could we step out into the hallway. I need to ask you some questions about your restaurant."

Downstairs, the little body of believers were leaving the hospital, confident their prayers had made a difference.

Phoebe made a quick exit, saying she had to get back to the store.

Mary Catherine checked her watch and realized she would be late in picking up Jill from daycare if she didn't hurry.

Tony suggested calling his mother and having her pick up Jill. "I think we should all go out to eat and celebrate our new sister."

"That sounds great! That is, if you're sure your mom won't care. I still have two free tickets to that new restaurant. That will pay for me and Lois," Mary added. "This will be great fun! Look how God is taking care of us!"

"Hey! I forgot about that. I have mine too," Tony said. "Shall we go in my car?"

"Do you think your mom will be disappointed?" Ellen asked.

"I'll call her."

Mary, Lois, and Ellen chatted excitedly while Tony went back into the hospital to use the pay phone. As he walked down the hall, he noticed Peter Ellington leaving the hospital with an important-looking gentleman. *Probably someone who works for his father,* Tony mused.

Looking a little subdued, Tony returned from his phone call. "My mom's already left the office, and the receptionist said she was going grocery shopping after she picked up Jen. I hate for her to miss out, but I'm sure she will want us to go without her."

"Well, if no one cares, I'll pick up Jill and meet you there," Mary suggested.

The other three agreed and left in Tony's car.

Mary picked up Jill and explained to her she had to be on her very best behavior because they were going to a very fancy grownup restaurant. Handing her keys to the valet, she wondered how much she would have to tip him after the meal. *I should just be thankful for the free meal,* she reminded herself.

<center>~~~</center>

Across town, Peter Ellington was amazed at the insinuation that his new restaurant could be involved in anything as diabolical as kidnapping. His confidence in Katrina was wavering until he saw Larry Grant across the room at the water cooler. Larry waved and smiled, assuring Peter that everything would be fine.

Everything's going to be okay, Peter said to himself. *Larry won't allow this to go too far without bending the truth to help me.*

"I think I've answered all your questions," Peter snapped. "I have a very sick wife back at the hospital. They don't expect her to live. The least I can do is be with her in her final moments."

Detective Layman looked chastised and dismissed him. As soon as Peter closed the door, Layman beckoned Grant over, "Assign a team to watch his every move. If I'm not mistaken, he's the kingpin right under Katrina. He's getting desperate, and desperate men make foolish mistakes."

Peter, his clothes wet with perspiration, swore quietly as he drove his Mercedes across town to Katrina's house. *She isn't going to like this. She*

266

isn't going to like this at all. He laid on the horn, calling the man in front of him a fool because he hesitated at the light. He couldn't help noting the bumper sticker spouted some sort of religious jargon.

Stupid fools...the world will be a better place once we've gotten rid of all of them. He swore again, and his eyes flashed angrily as he came to a screeching halt in front of Katrina's Victorian home. She was at the door and opened it before he stepped onto the massive porch.

"Well, did you do it?"

"I was stopped."

"How could that be?"

"They've called in the feds, that's how! You said they would never be able to trace this back to me. You said the spirits would protect me. You said..."

"Shut up! You simpering fool," she hollered. Then, in a lower tone, she cajoled him. "Peter, look into my eyes. You are calm, Peter, you are...very... calm."

He obeyed and was amazed at the peace he felt.

"There will be one more kidnapping, and this time the child will be sacrificed on the altar. The spirits will be appeased, and this thing will be over."

"But how can this work? Joan is dead or as good as, the feds have linked my restaurant to the kidnappings, the…"

"Shushhh," she whispered, placing her fingers on his lips. "Be still and obey the spirits. We don't have to know everything at once. They will lead us one step at a time."

The ringing telephone interrupted her instructions. She left the room to answer the phone but moments later returned, a look of triumph on her face.

"That was the restaurant calling," her eyes were glistening with glee. "The spirits are with us, Peter! We have the keys to both the Sands' and also to that Larson woman's house!" She laughed diabolically. "Don't you see, Peter? It's a sign! Don't you see? There's no way they would both show up at the restaurant tonight unless it was by our intervention. Our *Master* has arranged it. Don't you see? It's a sign. You don't have to be afraid. This is all going to work out for your good."

Chapter Forty-Four

Katrina began placing the phone calls as soon as Peter left. She carefully chose those who had proven to be the most loyal to her in the past. Only the core group would be invited to take part in this most sacred of all ceremonies. *I will call the Ravencrafts, the Higgbees, and, of course, Mrs. Musgrave, but not Larry Grant. I've felt uncomfortable around him lately. He says all the right words and yet…the spirits are warning me against him. He thinks I don't notice that disbelieving smirk on his face when I try to explain to him the incarnate birth of our promised savior. Lucifer must be born in the form of a man. How can Larry disregard the most sacred promise of all if he's one of us? No, he's not one of us. He's not to be trusted. If the plan is to work, if Lucifer is to come into global power, there is no time to waste. Joan has turned against us, but she'll be avenged. If I want to be used, the time is now. If I fail, there will be others to take my place. If I'm loyal, my reign will last throughout eternity.*

The message to each one she called was simple, "Meet at the farmhouse now." Katrina told Peter to retrieve one of the children and bring her at two o'clock. The sacrifice would be held at three.

~~~

Picking up the keys at the restaurant, he palmed them smiling. They were labeled with tiny circles of paper. One said Jen and the other said Jill. He held the keys in his hand. "Which one, which one," he whispered. Katrina told him to make the choice. He had told Joan she would have to make the choice. That was a big mistake. *I should have never trusted her. She wasn't ready. This is Katrina's fault. She should have known that Joan was too new to be trusted.*

Peter drove slowly back to his home and quietly unlocked the back door. The house was silent. It was after midnight and the servants were all asleep. He quickly changed into the black turtleneck shirt and the tight-fitting black pants he reserved for this special task. Glancing at his watch, he realized he should hurry. Putting both keys in his pocket, he drew one out. "Jill," he whispered. He'd driven past Mary Catherine's house earlier in the evening. The lights were on, and he saw Mary through the window just before she pulled the curtains. The room was wallpapered with pink and blue Teddy bears and was located on the front side of the house. He waited until he was sure all the lights were out and then parked his car in an alley two blocks away.

Peter never saw the two policemen watching his every move as he walked up to the porch. The key turned easily enough in the lock, and he carefully pushed on the door. It opened without a sound. Two inches open, and it stopped. A safety chain held it secure. Peter cursed softly under his breath and quietly walked back to his car. The two officers watching him let out a sigh at the same time.

Four miles across town, Peter looked at the clock on the dashboard. No time to lose, and yet he couldn't risk speeding. This was the place. He was sure of it. Yes, there on the mailbox it said 'Anthony Sands'. *This neighborhood is very dark, that's good,* he thought as he silently walked up to the front door.

Placing the key in the lock, he turned it. His heart was beating wildly as he pushed it open. "No safety chain here," he whispered. Leaving the door slightly ajar, he tiptoed into the house. For a moment he stood motionless and called on the spirits to work through him. As his eyes grew accustomed to the dim light, he saw the hallway to the left. These ranch-style houses were all laid out in a similar blueprint. A nightlight in the hall softly illuminated two closed doors and one partially open. Staying close to the wall, he slid silently toward the open door. He could see the corner of a dollhouse from where he was standing by the light of a nightlight. Moving closer, he peered around the door. Yes, there she lay in her little bed. *This is almost too easy. The spirits are certainly helping me tonight.* He almost laughed as he took the bottle of chloroform out of his pocket. Pouring a small amount onto his handkerchief, he headed toward the child's room.

~~~

Jennifer stirred uneasily in her sleep. Someone was shaking her awake.

"Daddy?" she mumbled softly. Someone was whispering in her ear, "You are safe, Jennifer, don't be afraid, I've been sent to protect you. Just call for your Daddy."

Wide awake now, she sat up in bed, rubbed her eyes, and tried to determine if she was dreaming. There on the end of her bed sat a man all dressed in white. He smiled at her reassuringly. In the doorway stood another man holding a cloth and a small bottle. He was dressed all in black. She looked back at the man dressed in white. He whispered, "It's okay, Jennifer, you don't have to be afraid. I'll keep you safe until your daddy comes.

272

Now use your big girl voice and call for your daddy as loud as you can."

Jennifer yelled, "DADDY!"

The man in black seemed to be frozen in place. He frowned and his face contorted as Jennifer yelled repeatedly, "DADDY...DADDY, HELP ME!"

Two doors opened simultaneously as Tony and his mother both rushed from their bedrooms toward Jennifer. Judy saw Peter first and screamed. Tony, behind her, pushed past, practically knocking her to the ground. Peter continued staring straight ahead at the white being that was seated at the foot of Jennifer's bed. In a matter of three seconds, Tony punched Peter, first in the stomach and then in the jaw, crumpling him to the ground.

Hearing Judy's scream, the two police officers following Peter rushed in the open door. Guns drawn, they stood behind Judy, viewing the unconscious Peter who was sprawled on the hallway floor.

Tony scooped Jennifer up out of her bed, hugging her with all of his might and whispering, "Baby, Baby...are you alright? Are you alright?"

"I'm okay, Daddy," Jennifer said, patting Tony's neck. "The man in the white clothes kept me safe."

Judy placed her arms around her son and granddaughter, and while hugging them with all her might, she asked, "What man in the white clothes, Sweetie?"

Jennifer looked back at the bed surprised to find her protector was no longer in the room.

"I guess he had to go home," she said.

"I guess so," Tony agreed and gave his mom a baffled look over Jen's head.

"An angel?" Judy mouthed silently.

Tony shook his head slowly in bewilderment and questioned, "Could it be?"

Chapter Forty-Five

In the secret room beneath the farmhouse, Katrina, dressed in her ceremonial robe of red velvet, passed the glasses of wine laced with hallucinogenic drugs.

Row upon row of candles lined the walls, illuminating the satanic symbols and carvings that decorated the walls. The fire in the fire pit was lit, and the flames roared higher and higher as Katrina circled the firepit, calling on the gods of the ages to come and inhabit them. "Come Dagon, come Beelzebub, come Moloch, and come Baal. Come and inhabit our very being," she cried.

With upraised hands, she began to chant her incantations. Someone to the side began to play a rhythmic beat on a drum. The chanting became a song and then a dance, and the worshipers began to whirl in wild abandon.

Katrina periodically glanced toward the stairway expectantly. *Any moment now, Peter will arrive with the child. It is nearing three o'clock.* She thought in disgust, *Where is he?*

Throwing more chemicals into the fire to cause a higher, more brilliant flame, she began to prophesy at the top of her lungs while continuing to whirl around the fire.

One of the women came staggering toward Katrina, her eyes wild, her mouth foaming. She spoke in a guttural voice, "Take me, take me. Let me be the sacrifice." She threw herself at Katrina's feet, almost knocking Katrina into the fire pit. Stepping backward to avoid her, Katrina didn't notice that the hem of her cape dipped into the flaming fire pit and began to smolder.

Unaware of the danger, she paced back and forth as the small crowd watched, fascinated by the flaming garment that was trailing behind her. The Oriental rug with the ornately embroidered pentagon was the first to catch fire. Still, she whirled and chanted, her eyes closed for better concentration. Next, the red carpet beneath the rug burst into flame. Before she realized what was happening, the tapestries and heavy draperies on the walls had also begun to blaze.

At first, the dancers viewed the fire as a wonderful display of their leader's power. Now horrified and confused by the drugs, the dancers tried to make their way to the exit at the top of the stairs only to find the door was locked. Katrina had not wanted to risk any interruptions during this, the most sacrilegious of all incantations. She had locked the door, knowing Peter had the only other key and would be arriving shortly with the child.

Within moments, Katrina was overcome by smoke inhalation. She fell and lay crumpled in the center of the room, the key held tightly in her hand while the others piled at the top of the stairs pounding on the door and begging for someone to let them out, but all to no avail.

The end came quickly. The chemicals Katrina used to make the fire explosive during the ceremony were in storage behind the curtain that hung much too close to the altar. In a matter of moments, they were ignited. Gas pipes were jarred loose in the first explosion allowing gas to feed the already raging fire. In moments, the house was blown to pieces, leaving nothing but a burning inferno.

In an instant, all the plans of Katrina Polworth were aborted. She had failed in her great endeavor to bring forth the Anti-Christ.

Sirens screamed toward the farmhouse as fire trucks arrived, but to the firemen's amazement, there was only a deep flaming hole where the farmhouse had once stood.

Marvin Payne was driving the first truck to arrive. He had been a fireman for over twenty years but had never seen anything even closely resembling the hole of fire. Robert Hughes drove one of the emergency vehicles. He edged toward

Marvin, speaking in awe. "Looks like the mouth of Hell opened up," he whispered.

"I know," Robert said in awe.

"Do you think there was anyone in there?"

"Well, from the looks of all the cars parked out front, I'd say quite a few. There's nothing we can do for the poor buggers now," he said, wiping tears away with the back of his hand.

"I wonder why they didn't run out. There's nobody around."

"We may never know. It looks like maybe a gas line explosion. If it was, they didn't have time to think about getting out."

"It's going to be hard to identify the bodies."

"We'll probably be able to come up with some of the names from the car registrations."

"Do you think it was a party?"

"God only knows."

More fire trucks were coming from another county, their sirens blaring, their somber cry in the night, not realizing there was nothing that could be done. The rescue workers stood around the burning hole, hats in hand to show respect. Others gazed into the hole mesmerized. Some cried silently for the victims who were beyond help.

"Sometimes I hate this job, Robert. You know what I mean?"

Robert just nodded mutely, continuing to stare into the fiery hole.

Chapter Forty-Six

Mary Catherine wasn't sure if she first felt the house shake, or if she was awakened by the boom. Her immediate thought was an earthquake. Waking out of a sound sleep, she reached for the light switch on the lamp bedside her bed. Blurry-eyed, she looked at the clock. *I wonder what's going on. We don't have earthquakes in Indiana. Could that have been an explosion? What on earth is happening?*

Shortly after she awoke, she heard sirens sounding in the distance. Just as she decided to turn the light off and try to go back to sleep, the telephone rang. Ellen's excited voice started questioning before she could say hello.

"Are you okay?"

"Yes, why, what's happening," she asked sleepily.

"Tony just caught the kidnapper."

"What!" Mary sat up in bed wide awake.

"Mary, it was Peter."

"Peter Ellington?"

"I'm afraid so."

"But…why? Why would he do such a thing?"

"I don't know, but Mary…the police said he tried to break into your house before he broke into Tony's."

"What!" Mary was instantly on her feet. She looked down at Jill who was still sleeping peacefully beside her."

"Is Jill ok?"

"She's right here with me. I put her in my bed last night after she had a nightmare. But Ellen, what about Tony? I can't believe all of this. How did he catch him?" Mary sat back down on the bed beside Jill and pulled the covers up around her.

"I don't know all the details. I woke up to the police sirens and the police lights flashing in my bedroom window. I grabbed my robe and ran across the street, arriving just in time to see them taking Peter Ellington away in handcuffs. It was so weird, he just kept repeating, "Call Katrina Polworth. She'll explain everything."

"How are Jennifer and Tony? And…oh my, how is Judy? I just can't believe any of this. Is everybody okay?"

"Yes, thankfully everyone is okay, but that's not all. The story gets even more bizarre. Jennifer said an angel woke her and stayed with her until her daddy caught the bad man."

"An angel?"

"Yes, she said he was a man wearing bright white clothes that looked like sunshine, and it made her happy just to look at him. She said he had a wonderful smile, but he disappeared after the bad man was caught."

"And she's not traumatized?"

"Tony said she seems pretty calm, happy actually, and she sure is proud of her daddy."

"What? I mean how did he rescue her?"

"I guess he punched Peter out."

"Oh my! I wonder if Joan knew about this…about Peter, that is…and what about Lois?"

"I'm right here, Mary," Lois said into the extension. "Ellen told me to get on the other phone. All we know is Tony just left to go down to the station to give a statement. I'm going to stay with Judy until Tony gets back, but we wanted to make sure you and Jill were all right first. We heard this explosion, and well, this sure is turning out to be some kind of a creepy nightmare."

"Ellen, could you come over?" Mary asked. "Unless you think you need to go with Lois."

"I'll be right there. I don't think any of us will be able to go back to sleep tonight. Wait a minute…do you hear those sirens? It sounds like more fire trucks. I wonder what's going on now?"

"I can't hear them over here, but you're closer to the fire station. I did hear sirens earlier," Mary said. "I don't know if it was fire trucks or police cars, but…"

"I'm hanging up now," Lois interrupted. "I think somebody should be with Judy and Jen."

"Okay, thanks for calling me. Are you coming, Ellen?"

"I'll be there as soon as I get some clothes on."

Mary hung up the phone and walked into the living room. Sure enough, the door was ajar. She caught her breath and started trembling as she realized she had only installed the chain yesterday. "Thank you, God, thank you," she said, closing the door and turning the lock.

"Please, Father, help Judy," she prayed as she dialed her number. Judy picked up on the first ring. "Judy? It's Mary Catherine. Are you okay?"

Amazingly, Judy sounded excited, and not frightened or traumatized at all. "Oh, Mary! You just won't believe what happened. Tony caught the kidnapper!"

"Tell me about it?"

"Well, last week after we went to your Bible study, Pastor Wind said he'd lost sight of the importance of prayer, so, Pastor, Evelyn, and I started a prayer group. Last night was our first meeting. We only had ten attending, but we all prayed that the child abductor would be caught and...and...can you believe it! This very night my Tony caught him!"

"Wow, that's amazing!"

"I'm so sorry I called you and Ellen fanatics. Isn't this the most wonderful thing? And Mary, you won't believe this, but our little Jennifer saw an angel! Can you believe it? I know it's hard to understand, but there isn't any other explanation! I said to Tony maybe she was dreaming about an angel before that man came into her room, but Tony said when Peter got in the police car, he kept asking about the man in the white suit."

"It sounds like a miracle right out of the Bible," Mary laughed. "This is so wonderful!"

"Can you believe it? We just prayed one time and all these wonderful things happened! It's not like I never prayed before," she chuckled. "It's just that we got serious about prayer. You know, prayed from our heart. Pastor says it's not enough to just pray at church or to pray memorized prayers. We need to talk to God about everything. Oh my, this is all so new to me, but isn't it exciting! I have cold chills just talking about it!"

"I'll have to admit, this is new to me too, but it is the most exciting thing I've ever heard of!"

"I've gone to church all my life and I guess, I guess, I just thought God's in charge, so why bother Him?"

"I think a lot of people have that misconception."

"I never realized how important it is to pray for everything. Why, I think I was practically an unbelieving believer. Oh…I must go. I think Lois is at the door. I have to tell her all about what happened. Oh Mary, I'm just so excited. I'll talk to you more about this tomorrow."

Mary Catherine smiled. She wasn't even tempted to say, 'Well others have been praying too.' She thought it but bit her tongue, rejoicing with Judy over her new revelation of God's love and goodness.

Hanging up the phone, Mary whispered her thanksgiving. "Thank you, Lord. You are so good, and you are so faithful to partner with us even in our smallest endeavors. I know you haven't forgotten Abigail. Please, Lord Jesus, watch over our little Abby wherever she is and bring her safely back to us."

Hearing Ellen at the door, she ran to let her in.

Chapter Forty-Seven

Larry's mind was bombarded with questions as he nosed his squad car toward home. Why did Katrina blow up the entire group of Satan worshipers, or did she? Was it possible that she had blown up the entire cult to cover her tracks and she escaped? *I'll have to wait for the report on the dental records.*

He still couldn't quite believe it. He knew the names of most of the core people but would have to wait and see if the numbers on the car registrations matched up with the number of bodies.

The sun was shining brightly as he made his way toward home. It promised to be a sizzler of a day. He made a mental note, *Next week is Independence Day.* He groaned and then remembered Abby. *The first thing is to let her out and explain what happened. I hope she's okay. She could probably press charges against me and the entire police department.*

Somehow, I'll have to explain how necessary it was to keep her there for her protection, and my protection too. It looks like no one else on the force was involved. I pray she'll understand there was no way I could be sure who was involved or who would blow my cover. Thank God, it looks like anyone who would have done her harm is either dead or in jail. Marilyn Musgrave's Buick was parked at the farmhouse, so I imagine she's gone.

Leaning forward in the seat, Larry tried to get the kinks out of his back. He hadn't slept in over forty-eight hours, and he was beginning to feel it. Waking the mayor with the good news, he had received a verbal pat on the back. Now he longed for a hot shower and cool sheets. *Maybe I could get Mrs. Kelly to set Abby free. It's sure tempting, no, I can't do that to her. I owe her an explanation and an apology, but first I need a shower...another hour in that place won't hurt her.*

Larry pulled into his mom's driveway, slid from beneath the steering wheel, and walked laboriously up the steps of the back porch. Opening the familiar screen door, he found his mom and Mrs. Kelly sitting at the kitchen table with a third person. She had her back to the door but looked strangely familiar. The three women were drinking coffee in animated conversation. They all stopped as he entered. Elva Grant gave a little yelp of joy and rushed to his side.

"Larry! Oh, thank God, you're okay! We heard the sirens, and then they were talking about an explosion on the radio. What happened?"

"We haven't sorted it all out yet, but it looks like everything in Katrina Polworth's kingdom is coming down. They caught the kidnapper last night, and it was Peter Ellington."

"No...I can't believe it!"

"And the explosion was at Peter's farmhouse. The fire department says it was most likely a gas leak. I can't tell you much more, just that Peter Ellington was right under Katrina in the power structure. I'm afraid most of the people involved in the cult were killed in the explosion."

The young woman at the table still had her back to him, but there was something... "Abigail MacDonald?" he whispered.

She slowly turned, made eye contact, and gave him a glaring stare.

"Oh, thank goodness you released her," he said, addressing Mrs. Kelly.

Abby turned toward Larry, continuing to glare at him in anger. "I can't believe you!" she spit at him. "You have...put...me...through...HELL for the last few days...and all you can say is..."

Larry looked back at her and sighed heavily as he tried to think of an answer.

Abby was trying to compose herself, but her frustration was giving way to angry tears. When he didn't answer her, she lashed out at him again. "Why didn't you bring me *here* in the first place, instead of compromising my sanity by locking me in that jail cell? I wasn't the criminal, or did you forget!"

Larry shook his head slowly. "I'm sorry…I'm so very sorry…this wasn't a normal case. We weren't dealing with normal people," he said, trying to explain.

"Well, I'm sorry too!" she said sarcastically. "I guess I had the mistaken idea that murders were all *normal*, except of course for your special brand!" Her eyes were flashing fire, and Larry looked helplessly at his mother, beseeching her help.

Elva Grant gave him an ' I told you so' look, and setting her lips in a firm line, said nothing.

"Why did you bring her here, Mrs. Kelly? How did you know the danger was over?"

Abby jumped in before Mrs. Kelly could answer. "She didn't bring me here. I escaped, but you could have spared me days of fear and discomfort if you'd only explained what was happening."

Larry tried once more to voice an apology. "You're right, and I'm truly sorry. I didn't handle any of this well." He suddenly saw Abby as a small, wounded child, and he was ashamed of the heartless way he'd treated her. "I…I didn't mean to keep you in that hole, I mean…in the beginning, it was a temporary arrangement. I planned on moving you as soon as I could figure out what to do with you, but then I got so involved in the case I…I, well, I'm very sorry. I realize I have a lot of explaining to do. Please forgive me. I guess…I thought I gave Mrs. Kelly instructions to explain everything."

Her initial anger spent, Abby replied, "Your Mom just now filled me in on most of it," Abby said, sighing as she quietly blew her nose and tried to compose herself. "And no, you did NOT tell Mrs. Kelly to tell me anything." She sighed again. "And…and…you locked me up like I was the criminal."

"I'm so sorry, Abby and Mrs. Kelly, I owe you both an apology. I told you what to do in the beginning, but then I never checked back with you to make sure you were able to explain what was going on."

"I didn't know what was going on!" Mrs. Kelly responded innocently.

"Yes, I know," he said. Taking her weathered hand, he patted it affectionately. Then looking at Abby he said, "Now, can you please tell me how you ended up in our kitchen?"

Abby sighed, "If you had only filled me in, I would have stayed put. I thought you were as evil as Marilyn Musgrave."

Larry tried to hold back a smile. Even though exasperated, frustrated, and angry, she was so cute and funny, and he admired her spunk.

"Continue," he smiled kindly.

Abby couldn't help herself. She could feel her anger dissipating, and she smiled back shyly. "Okay, I managed to crawl through the vent in the ceiling."

Larry raised his eyebrows in surprise at her tenacity but remained silent.

"I had no idea I was in the bridal shop basement. When I got to the cellar level, the door was locked from the outside, but I managed to climb up the coal shoot and escape. I was terrified when I realized I was in the backyard of the bridal shop, especially when I heard the explosion and then all of the sirens that were going off. They seemed to be sounding from everywhere, and I didn't know what was happening or where I should go.

"But how did you get here?" he frowned.

"As soon as I squeezed through the little door, and realized where I was. I panicked and started running. I hadn't run very far when I fell." She pointed to a nasty-looking skinned knee showing through a tear in her sweatpants. "I was sitting on the curb crying when a kind lady in a white car pulled over and asked me if I needed help. I guess I looked pitiful. I was not only crying but I was covered with coal dust with blood running down my leg." She looked over at Larry's mom for affirmation. "I was afraid to trust anyone," Abby motioned toward Larry's mother, "but this lady looked so concerned for my welfare that I decided to risk it."

"And it was you, Mom?"

Elva Grant smiled and nodded.

And Abby continued, "I asked her if she could take me to the police station, and she told me to 'get in.' Something inside of me broke, and I just started crying and telling her everything I'd gone through. I was half-afraid she would think I was a lunatic, but…"

"Here's my part," Elva interrupted. "I woke up and I couldn't seem to stop praying. When I heard the sirens, I started praying for you of course," she nodded toward Larry. "But then I started praying for the girl in the bomb cellar. About daylight, I got up, dressed, and decided to drive to the coffee shop and get some donuts."

"But how did you know it was Abby?" Tony asked.

"I didn't, but I could tell whoever she was, she was in trouble. Our prayer group was praying for her, so I thought it could be her, but I couldn't imagine why she would be sitting alongside the road."

Larry listened expectantly.

"When she told me what happened to her, I told her who I was and what I knew. It seemed…well…that she would understand once she knew you could be in danger if she showed up at the police station."

Larry hung his head, "I've been too afraid to trust God or anyone," he sighed. "Abby, can you ever forgive me?"

Abby closed her eyes and sighed heavily. "Yes, if I can just go home. I…I'm so tired and I'm ready for this to all be over."

Larry stood, "Your car is in our garage, but you might want to make some phone calls first. Your friends need to know you're okay."

Abby made the phone call to Ellen at once, who screamed, "Glory Halleluiah!" at the sound of Abby's voice and then began to cry. It was hard for either girl to make heads or tails out of what each was saying, as they were both so excited that they kept interrupting each other. Finally, Abby asked Ellen to please call everyone and tell them she would be home in a matter of minutes. As she hung up the phone, Larry stepped forward.

"Are you sure you're alright to drive? I mean, after all you've been through, you look exhausted. I'll be happy to drive you. My mom can drive your car home for you and ride back with me."

A wave of gratitude swept over her. "Thank you, but I know you're tired too. Are you sure you want to do this?"

"I think under the circumstances, it's the least I can do."

As she rode along in the squad car, she closed her eyes and silently thanked God for all He had brought her through. *I wish I'd trusted you a long time ago, Lord. Please, God, help Larry Grant put an end to all this evil.*

She was sound asleep and snoring softly before Larry had gone a mile and was yet to find out her prayer had already been answered. But it was not Larry who had put an end to Satan's plans. A badge, a gun, not even the F.B.I. could stop the tide of darkness that had overshadowed the little town. Instead, a handful of faithful prayers, partnering with God, had accomplished what no lawman could do.

Chapter Forty-Eight

At seven-forty-five in the morning, the pop, pop, pop of gunfire woke Ellen out of a sound sleep. Her heart beat wildly at first, and then she remembered it was the Fourth of July, and what she heard was not gunfire, but firecrackers. She moaned, covered her head with a pillow, and wondered briefly, *What parent in their right mind would permit their child to…*

"Of course," she jumped out of bed, pulled on her robe, peered out the window, and grinned at the confirmation of her suspicion.

Across the street, sitting in a lawn chair in the driveway, Tony was setting off firecrackers. Jen, whose eyes were scrunched up tightly, had her fingers placed securely in her ears. After each explosion, she would laugh and clap her hands in glee.

Ellen could hear one of her housemates in the shower down the hall as she made her way to the kitchen to start the coffee. Abby was already up, dressed, and sitting at the kitchen table eating toast and reading the paper. "Well, I guess it's finally over," she sighed and held up the paper pointing to the headline.

Abducted Children Returned to Their Parents.

Ellen started filling the coffee pot in the sink. "I hate to think what they've been through." She shuddered as she realized how close this evil had come to the children she loved. "We have a lot to celebrate today, Abby."

"Yes, and I for one am going to enjoy every moment."

"Our neighbors seem to have gotten an early start on the celebration." The joyful look on Ellen's face increased as another pop, pop, pop, pop resonated.

"Larry has to work at the parade this morning, but he said he'll be by this afternoon for the cookout."

"Oh, so now it's Larry and not Sergeant Grant?"

"You know he keeps checking on me." Abby blushed. "Despite all he put me through, he really is a very nice man. In fact, he has already called this morning."

"I think he's nice too," Ellen affirmed.

"And…well, I understand he was trying to protect me, so I've forgiven him."

295

"That's very gracious of you," Ellen smiled.

"Remember at the last cookout, when you told me God could make something good out of the worst of circumstances?"

"Yes."

"Well, he has," she said simply. "I think Larry is one of the kindest most sincere men I've ever met and…"

The doorbell rang, interrupting their conversation. Tony and Jen stood on the step, both smiling mischievously.

"Come watch Daddy light sparkles," Jen said, holding up the box for Ellen to see.

"I thought sparklers were for after dark."

"We can't wait…right Daddy?"

Ellen laughed, "I haven't had my coffee, and I'm not even dressed."

Tony looked at his watch, "We'll give you twenty minutes."

"Okay then, you better leave so I can meet my deadline."

Lois peeked around the corner, still in her robe. "Is everybody gone? Oh good, you made coffee."

"Oh dear, I promised Tony I'd be over in twenty minutes, and if I do, I'll be leaving you with all the preparation for the cookout."

"Are you kidding? I love doing this. Go…go…get out of here…scoot," Lois said.

"I can help," Abby volunteered.

"Okay, you start on the baked beans. I'll be back as soon as I throw some clothes on, and Abby?"

"Yes?"

"It sure is wonderful to have you back!"

~~~

"I can't believe your mom is riding on the church float!" Ellen said gleefully.

Tony laughed. "I can't believe she volunteered to be the Statue of Liberty!"

"I sure hope her arm doesn't get tired holding that torch up all morning," Abby added.

"We're going to the parade," Jen announced. "Want to come with us?"

"Yes, I do. I wouldn't miss it!"

Jen twirled round and round dancing in front of them. Tony and Ellen sat side-by-side on the porch swing, swinging lazily in the early morning heat. Tony stopped the swing and turned to Ellen as he lit another sparkler and gently warned Jen not to touch it or get too close. "You know, I don't think I've ever been happier," he smiled.

"Me too," she said, watching Jen, afraid to look at Tony, afraid her eyes would betray her feelings.

The sparkler fizzled to a stop, and he placed it carefully back in the box and took her hand. He looked straight ahead for a moment, and then unexpectedly leaned over and kissed her. It was so soft and quick, almost like it hadn't happened. She tingled from head to toe, and she felt a bit light-headed.

"Light another one, Daddy?"

Ellen was thinking the same thing. Her thoughts made her blush.

"Ellen...I don't have a ring...things have been so...so...well, I guess this isn't very romantic, I mean, we aren't even alone...but Ellen...I can't wait any longer to tell you how much I love you. I haven't had you out of my mind for more than two minutes since the first time I saw you. Oh shoot...I'm going about this all wrong. Ellen, will you...could you even consider...what I'm trying to say is...I don't want to ever let you go. Would you even consider marrying someone like me?"

To Tony's surprise, Ellen covered her face with her hands and started to cry.

"Oh, Ellen...I'm so sorry. Please forgive me. I should have waited, I should have taken you to a nice restaurant, brought flowers, and already had a ring picked out...it's just that...well...you look so beautiful sitting there, and I'm so happy just to be here with you and...and..."

"Tony, I'm not crying in disappointment! I'm just so happy! I don't need a restaurant, or flowers, or even a ring. I just need you and Jen!"

This time Tony took her in his arms and gave her a kiss that made the sparkler dim in comparison. They pulled apart breathlessly to a wide-eyed Jennifer watching in bewilderment. "Are we getting married, Daddy?"

"Would you like that, Pumpkin?"

Jennifer pushed her little body between Ellen and Tony and snuggled under their intertwined arms. Nodding her head 'yes' to Tony's question, she looked thoughtfully at Ellen. "Will you be my mommy, Ellen?"

"I would love to be your mommy, honey, if you want me to be."

"I do," she said. That settled, Jennifer pushed away from the group hug. "Light another sparkler, Daddy!"

"How about two this time, one for each hand?"

Jennifer twirled and danced around them, jumping and laughing as Tony swooped dramatically, making figure eights with the fiery sticks.

"Wahoo! I'm doing that on the inside," Ellen said as she clapped her hands and watched the two of them twirl.

"Join us," he said, his voice husky with emotion as he lit two more sparklers and handed them to Ellen.

For the rest of my life, she thought. Too overcome with joy to even speak, she reached for the starry sticks.

Chapter Forty-Nine

It's been four weeks!" Joan pouted sullenly. "When do I get these bandages off? I feel like an Egyptian mummy."

"The doctors say you're making remarkable progress," answered Mary Catherine, "and they say you'll probably have very little scarring."

Joan turned her face toward the wall, ignoring the chocolate milkshake Mary was trying to tempt her with.

Ellen was arranging the roses she had brought and was trying very hard not to respond to Joan's childish outburst. Mary gave Ellen a troubled look and tried again.

"We don't want to bother you, Joan. We just wanted you to know that we're here for you. We love you and we trust that you'll make a full recovery."

"Listen, you guys, I know you mean well, but if you think all of this attention is going to get me to change…well, think again. I had religion crammed down my throat for as long as I can remember. What has God ever done for me?"

"Well, for one thing, you weren't at the farmhouse when it exploded. And you didn't die in the car crash," Ellen said as she fussed with the flowers.

"And the doctors are calling your recovery a miracle," Mary Catherine added.

"And you aren't going to jail if you turn states evidence. That sure is something to be thankful for," Ellen smiled.

"But how can I thank God when I didn't pray for any of those things," Joan sputtered.

"I did," Mary Catherine and Ellen said in unison.

"How can you say that you prayed for me? You had no idea what I was caught up in. I didn't even realize it myself until it was too late."

"We saw you were in spiritual trouble, and we prayed that somehow you would see the truth. We didn't need to know the details of your life to see that you were going in the wrong direction. We've been praying God would help you to see how much He loves you," Ellen said.

"I just wanted you to realize you could change," Mary Catherine added.

"Why do you think I want to change?"

Mary took a deep breath and plunged into the truth. "Because you always seemed to be angry, and I know that when I'm angry, it's because down deep I'm scared. I've found so much peace since I surrendered my life to Jesus. I just wanted that same thing for you."

"Okay," Joan conceded, "but it's different for you. You don't have all the baggage I grew up with. You don't know what it's like to have a father who beat you within an inch of your life with one hand and held the Bible in the other."

Mary Catherine took the lid off the milkshake and handed Joan a spoon, "Here try this. It's your favorite."

As Joan spoke, Mary remembered graphically how it was to grow up in her home where there was constant fighting. A *home where I never felt loved. At first, I thought the angry voices in the night were the worst that could happen, the angry words, the muffled crying. It seemed anything would be better than my mother's tears, but I was wrong. The worst was yet to come. The silence that followed my father leaving was worse than the crying. The silence of my mother sitting at the kitchen table staring into her own world, surrendering to the darkness that captured her soul for so many years.*

"I had a bad childhood too," Mary whispered.

"Oh sure, and I bet you had a stepmother that was mean to you too," Joan scoffed.

"Actually, I did."

Joan looked up surprised, "Really?"

303

"There was a time when I was filled with so much resentment toward my stepmother." Mary dropped her eyes. "I wanted her dead and...I thought I could never forgive her."

"Because..."

"I could give a lot of reasons, but for one, I was only twelve years old, but it was my dad's birthday so I asked my mom if I could do something special. It was March and still cold. I baked him a cake for his birthday. I really wanted his approval. He never had much time for me after he divorced my mother and remarried." Mary looked pensive remembering the pain.

"And..."

Mary took a deep breath, "I walked nearly three miles across town in the freezing rain to give him a cake I had baked, and when I got there, his new wife wouldn't let me in the house."

"The witch..."

"Yes, that's how I felt for a long time. She told me to take my mother's cake and go home. I couldn't convince her I had baked it. I was crying so hard I didn't realize how slippery the porch was until I slipped on the ice-covered porch and dropped the cake. I skinned my chin, and it was bleeding, but she just laughed at me."

"I hope she got hers. People like that deserve a special kind of hell."

"Well, actually, she did...kind of anyway. She always called my mother a lunatic...but in her old age, my stepmother lost her mind and now she's in a mental institution."

"Okay, I guess you have had your problems too. I'm sorry."

"It was a long time ago," Mary whispered, "and God has helped me to forgive her."

Joan sighed hugely and took the chocolate shake from Mary. "I still don't understand you guys. Why should any of you care about me? I sure haven't cared anything about you?"

"We feel like we're all kind of in the same boat. We didn't do anything to deserve God's forgiveness, but he forgave us anyway. He told us we should forgive and love in the same way He does. Not that it's always easy," Ellen said.

Joan gave a half smile and took a big spoonful of the ice cream. It was the first hint of acceptance Joan had shown to either of them. "Okay, I have to admit you've given me a lot to think about. But let's drop the sappy God stuff, at least for tonight."

As Joan looked towards the door, her total countenance changed, "Johnny!" she squealed in delight.

John Elwood stood in the doorway, a huge box of candy under one arm and flowers in the other. "Can I interrupt this girl talk?" he asked, blushing.

"Actually, we were just leaving, right Mary?" Ellen motioned toward the door and hurried Mary Catherine out of the room. Catching the elevator just as it was closing, the two started down.

"You have to say one thing for her, she has barely decided to divorce one before she has another one lined up," Ellen whispered.

"I feel sorry for her," Mary Catherine said. "I think she's covering up a lot of pain with her bravado. Joan is probably a lot more miserable than any of us can imagine. I don't think she's as hard as she pretends to be."

"I'm sorry, Mary. I guess I shouldn't judge her after all that's happened to her, but you've gone through a lot too, and you aren't bitter."

"I've not talked about it, but I have had to choose to forgive and it hasn't always been easy."

"Every time I'm around Joan, I end up getting mad and having to repent. I guess I just don't understand her. Just thinking about her gets me all wound up."

Mary smiled, "Maybe we should change the subject. How are the wedding plans coming along?"

"We're thinking about an autumn wedding."

"I love the fall. That sounds perfect."

Maybe October, of course, that doesn't give me much time to prepare. But hey, after all, I make wedding dresses for a living! I should be able to whip up a dress, don't you think."

The elevator opened on the ground level and the two walked out. "Judy tells me you've decided to open your own shop. Now you'll be able to design wedding dresses and pursue your original dream."

"Yes," Ellen sighed, "but it's so scary. I'm just going to start by sewing from my room at the house. Eventually, I hope to rent a shop but for now…"

"But you said you already have two orders."

"Yes, and Joan even said she wants me to make her dress when she and John Elwood get married."

"Actually, I think you could do anything you set your mind to," Mary grinned.

"I hope you know I want you to stand up with me?"

"Oh, Ellen, I would be honored! I knew you asked Abby to be your maid of honor, but I never dreamed you would ask me. I've never been in a wedding, not counting my own, of course," she laughed.

"Jill and Jen are going to be the flower girls. It will be so much fun to make their dresses."

"Ellen, I have faith in you, but how are you going to get this all done by October?"

"Abby will help. We're both temporarily unemployed, you know."

"The way Larry Grant looks at her, I wouldn't be surprised if she won't be working on her own wedding dress soon."

"I know. Isn't that the strangest outcome? Who would think she would end up marrying someone who had her locked up for days."

The two laughed together easily. "You know what they say about truth being stranger than fiction," Mary said shaking her head.

Ellen noticed a melancholy in Mary's voice and added, "There could be someone for you too, Mary."

"Well, right now I'm only concentrating on having a healthy baby, and that can't come quick enough. This is a change of subject, but I wanted to ask you something."

"Yes?"

"Lois said that Katrina put curses on all of us for praying against her plans. Can that hurt us as believers?"

Ellen frowned and then said, "Well, according to the Bible, an underserved curse can never harm a believer. In fact, the Bible says it goes back to the person who placed it. We certainly never wanted things to go the way they did for Katrina Polworth, Marilyn Musgrave, or any of their followers. This may sound heartless, but knowing the way God is,

I'm sure they all had plenty of opportunities to repent, and yet we have to face the fact that there are consequences for rebellion."

Mary looked pensive.

"Did you ask me that because you're worried about the baby?"

"I guess I kind of was. Thank you. I've so much to learn."

Ellen smiled. "Yes, we all do, but Philip and Phoebe said the Bible tells us that God is faithful to bring us to maturity, that is if we want Him to."

"Yes, I guess we do have to want Him to, don't we. And I guess it has to be more than just wanting him to." She sighed, "We have to cooperate with Him and change when He shows us an area that needs changing. I think that's the hardest part. Thank goodness He never gives up on us."

"I'm with you on that one, thank goodness is right."

Chapter Fifty

She awoke in a cold sweat. Once again, the nightmare was there to torment her. Joan looked around the hospital room and breathed a sigh of relief. In the dream, she was with Katrina and Peter, and they were all running from the flames of fire, a horde of demonic faces leering and threatening her. Glancing over at the flowers John Elwood had left, she smiled. He was a good man and wanted to marry her, not knowing what she would look like after the remaining bandages were removed.

In the dim light, she tried to see the numbers on the clock. Two-twenty, the time when Katrina liked to start her meetings. Joan shivered involuntarily. *The ward is so quiet. Why am I restless? I've got to stop reliving the past. Katrina Polworth and Marlyn Musgrave are gone. Peter is locked away, and all the people who wanted to destroy me are dead or incarcerated.*

Rolling over, she grimaced in pain. Her leg was still not completely healed. Reliving the past day, her mind reeled. *I wonder if there could be* some truth in what Ellen and Mary Catherine were talking about. *The federal agent who took my statement was certainly kind about everything.*

"Was that because of You, God?" she whispered.

I don't understand why Mary Catherine and Ellen want to be my friend.

Rolling over again, she thought of the sorrow she'd seen on John Ellington's face when he stopped by the day before to apologize. *I can't help but feel sorry for him. He looks so confused, so broken. He gave Peter everything materially, but he never gave him any restrictions, guidelines, or spiritual instruction. Although not in the same ways, Peter's family was as dysfunctional as mine.*

Joan tried to go back to sleep, but her life whirled before her in tormenting accusation. *I guess Mary Catherine did have it as bad as I did, yet she seems so happy, so content, and she is so kind to me. Why? She should be thinking about herself! How is she going to take care of two kids without a husband or even the prospect of a husband? What was she talking about when she said God promised in the Bible to take care of the widows and orphans? She isn't a widow, and her kids aren't orphans. How come she thinks that verse applies to her? She made her own bad luck, and now she's trying to tell me she is a widow of circumstance, and her kids are orphans. What makes her think*

311

that you love her? She says you are good and that you've forgiven her of every bad and foolish thing she's ever done. That sure isn't the God I've ever known about. If that is real, but of course it's not, how can it be? Tears slipped down her face, dampening her bandages.

"God?" she whispered in the darkness. "I know we haven't been friends. I guess you know I've always hated you. I've blamed you for every bad thing in my life. Ellen says you only want good for me. I thought you were my enemy. I'm sure you already know I've decided to do everything my dad said you hated."

"Mary Catherine says she wasn't like me. She said she always tried to be good, but she still didn't have peace. Ellen says that's why Jesus came. She says Jesus became a man to pay the price of our sins. I've never understood about Jesus, but I guess if I can believe Satan can take the form of a man, I guess…I guess I can believe Your Son could come in a man's body." She stopped crying, amazed that the revelation suddenly was a reality to her.

"God, I do want to believe that your Son came in the flesh! I do want to believe that He died for me."

The tears stopped and Joan began to laugh. "I do…I do!" She said it again and again, and as she said each 'I do', she was reminded of her wedding.

312

"God, it's kind of like a marriage, isn't it? You ask me if I will take your Son, and I say I do!"

Joan couldn't believe how happy and free just whispering 'I do' out loud made her feel. Every time she said those two words, she felt lighter and lighter.

She began to weep as her manipulation and adulterous hate-filled lifestyle paraded before her. The lies and rage loomed large, but instead of trying to ignore them, she said the words again. "Please, God, I hate the person I am. Please forgive me. If you can do anything with my life, I give it all to you."

With each I do, Joan felt the heaviness and the anger that had held her captive begin to decimate.

The rest of the night was spent in the bliss of thankfulness. *God, I think I see. I finally understand what I never could see before. Thank you, God, for taking this mess of my life. Ellen said I can start fresh and new and clean, and I do want that. Thank you, God, for your forgiveness and my new life. I pledge to do whatever you call me to do.*

~~~

Early the next morning, the doctor, making his rounds, was amazed at the glowing optimistic Joan that greeted him.

"You're making remarkable progress," he said.

She studied the worried look on his face as he took her vitals.

"There seems to be a 'but' in that statement," she questioned.

"You've had severe internal injuries, Joan. I'm sorry to have to tell you this, but aside from a miracle, you'll never be able to conceive a child."

He waited for her response, but there was none. He was a bit confused. This news would be overwhelming to almost any woman, and yet she smiled. "It will be alright. I don't know how, but I have faith that everything is going to be alright."

~~~

After the doctor left, Joan called Ellen and shared what she had experienced in the night. Ellen shared the news and that afternoon Joan's hospital room was filled with well-wishers. Even Philip and Phoebe Brown were there. Mary and Ellen both shed tears of joy when Joan joyously shared her encounter with God and everything that had happened in the middle of the night.

Later that evening, Mary Catherine went into labor and gave birth to another beautiful little girl. Joan demanded to see the baby, and a nurse finally gave in and wheeled her down to the maternity ward.

Her eyes filled with tears as she saw the nametag. *Dana Joan Larson...I can't believe this...my selfish ambition almost culminated in the death of Mary Catherine's little girl...and yet, she's given my name to this precious baby.*

Mary Catherine walked slowly down the hall. Seeing Joan from a distance, she watched her for a while and then walked up to her wheelchair. "Should you be up?" Mary asked quietly.

"Should you?" Joan shot back at her.

Turning from Joan's annoyed retort, Mary chose to ignore the snappy reply and instead studied the beauty of her newborn daughter.

"She's beautiful, Mary, so fresh and innocent," Joan whispered.

"So are you," Mary Catherine answered. "It's God's way."

Joan sighed and slowly shook her head. "There are so many changes."

"Good changes," Mary smiled.

Joan continued to study the miracle on the other side of the glass and added, "I guess I'll be married to John soon. Did you know he asked me to marry him even though we don't know the outcome of some of my injuries?"

"Whoa...slow down," Mary giggled. "Have you asked God if this is His will for you?"

Joan frowned and gave Mary a flippant, "I know…I know…you don't have to go all religious on me…I pray."

Mary realized she had said too much. "I'm just learning this too," she whispered in a humble reply.

"Anyway, why in the world would God object to John? He goes to church, and you and Ellen agree he's a good man."

Mary sighed, "Forgive me, Joan, it's none of my business. It's between you and God." Walking back to her room, Mary prayed silently, *Please, Lord, protect Joan from herself. Phoebe Brown says even though our spirit is brand new, we still need our mind renewed by your Word. Please help me to learn this lesson and share it with Joan without sounding preachy and turning her off.*

All the next day, Mary Catherine's friends dropped by her hospital room with gifts and congratulations. Everyone celebrated not only the baby's birth but Joan's surrender to God.

As Tony and Ellen stood looking in the nursery window, she couldn't help but be misty-eyed. *Oh, Lord, this beautiful child is such a blessing. Was it only a few months ago that I asked you to use me to reach my friends? Tony, Abby, Lois, Mary Catherine, and now Joan. How can I ever be thankful enough?*

Ellen wiped the tears away with the back of her hand. Tony noticed and handed her his handkerchief. He was beginning to realize that his future wife often cried out of pure joy. He placed his arm around her protectively as they left the hospital and walked into the rainy night.

"Funny, I used to hate rain," she laughed, "but now I see it as God's way of refreshing the earth."

"I've recently realized we're both seeing things a lot differently, and just think, we're only beginning. I can't even imagine all the wonderful things God has in store for us!"

"I'm just amazed at how God brought us together. If I hadn't moved across the street from you, we would have probably never met."

"I was desperate for answers, but I'd given up on God. Who could have ever guessed my answers would come from someone as beautiful as you."

"And I thought I only moved in with Abby out of financial desperation," Ellen laughed.

"Yes, and here it was all part of God's plan!"

She turned her face up to his, inviting a kiss, not even minding the soft rain that was slowly soaking them, and said, "God's purposes are certainly good."

He held her tightly. "They certainly are," he whispered, "and I'm never letting them go."

Made in United States
Cleveland, OH
20 January 2025

13297443R00187